He Won't Go
A Novel by

Stacey Covington-Lee

ISBN – 978-1-7338811-4-2

Published by: SCL Novel Publications

Cover Design: The Final Wrap

Editor: Kiera J. Northington

Formatting/Typesetting: Trinity DeKane

Logo/Web Design: T McKenzie Media

Printed in the United States of America

Acknowledgement

I thank and acknowledge God in all things. I thank Him for the gifts He has bestowed upon me and pray that He finds my use of His gift acceptable with this novel. I hope He allows the words that I've written to touch someone. This book has been a long time coming and many obstacles came to deter the finishing of it. But God... Thank you, Father, for putting this on my heart, for guiding me, for keeping me. I love you, Lord.

I'd like to give a special shout of thanks to Pastor Allen Page and First Lady Gail Page for their friendship, prayers, counsel, and love. The insight and feedback you gave as it pertains to this novel was invaluable.

Dedication

This book is dedicated to my biggest fan, my best friend, my mother, Myrtice Ruth Covington.

09/15/1939 – 02/24/2021

Forever in my heart, still holding my hand.

Cassandra Smith (my Schmitty), you are still loved and still missed.

CHAPTER 1

Ryker hoped his return to small-town Georgia would be pretty uneventful, but his mother had other plans. She was so proud of her only child, and she bragged about him and his accomplishments every chance she got. When he graduated as the valedictorian of his high school class, she invited the entire church over to celebrate. When he accepted a full-ride scholarship to Stanford, she had it announced in church and insisted their pastor pray over him. And it took darn near the entire congregation to console her when he boarded the Greyhound bus that took him to Atlanta's Hartfield-Jackson International Airport. Her baby had left her, but now he was coming back, and she intended to celebrate.

Constance did everything she could think of to prepare for Ryker's return. Of course, she had seen her son since he took off for college, but it was always out in Irvine, California, the place he'd called home since obtaining his engineering degree. Ryker was passionate about his work and convincing him to come back south for a couple of weeks was like pulling teeth, but Constance had no shame. She played the guilt card until he caved. One thing Ryker couldn't stand was the thought that he was doing something to cause his mother a second of unhappiness or heartache. When Constance started sniffling and allowed him to hear the tears that were caught up in her throat, Ryker hung up the phone, made airline reservations, and sent his mother a screenshot of his travel itinerary. Constance

He Won't Go

knew it was wrong to manipulate him like that, but she didn't care. She wanted her son home, and she was over the moon to know he would be arriving any minute.

Ryker descended the escalator at the Atlanta airport and immediately spotted the driver holding a sign with his name on it. He smiled at the guy and handed off his luggage, but the smile was just a mask. Ryker loved his mother and always enjoyed his time with her, but if he never had to go back to Allentown again, it would've been fine with him. He had fond memories of growing up in the country, but the most overpowering memory was that of his father's death. His beaten and bloodied body being laid out on their couch by the towns men that found him. The stifling heat in the country church during his funeral as the choir sang his soul home, the burial in the small cemetery in the back of the church, it was what Ryker had always wanted to escape. The thought of returning held no pleasure for him at all. But this trip was for his mother, and for her, nothing was off limits.

As the Escalade turned the corner onto his mom's street, all Ryker could do was drop his head and chuckle. He knew Constance would go all out, but the street was literally decorated with streamers and balloons. People he hadn't seen in years and others he'd never met cheered as the SUV slowly made its way down the road. The grills were smoking with the south's finest barbeque, and music filled the air. Just as he'd suspected, Constance had taken his homecoming celebration way too far.

"I'm sorry, sir," the driver interrupted Ryker's train of thought. "Did I miss something, are you a big star I failed to recognize?"

"Nah, man, I'm just a small-town boy coming home to visit his mom."

"Humph, my mama has never cared this much about my coming home," the driver chuckled.

"I wish mine didn't care as much either."

As the SUV came to a stop, Ryker began to rifle through his pocket for some cash. He wanted to tip the driver well for the pleasant two-hour drive from Atlanta to Allentown. The driver unloaded the luggage and was more than pleased when Ryker slid him two one-hundred-dollar bills. The driver tipped his hat, thanked Ryker, and backed his way out of the carnival happening on Oak Street.

"I can't believe my baby boy is finally home. I've been waiting so long for this day to arrive. You're back where you belong, son, you're back where you belong," Constance cried as she hugged and kissed Ryker as if he were just returning from war.

"It's good to be back, Mama," he lied as he wrapped his arms around Constance and lifted her into a tight bear hug. "I'm sorry I stayed away so long, but I promise we'll have a nice visit."

The day was filled with introductions, getting reacquainted with old friends and family member, and plenty of good food. The party lasted well into the night and by the time the last guest left, and last bag of trash was gathered, Ryker was wiped out. All he wanted was to shower and get some sleep. He'd almost forgotten how draining the high humidity of the county air could be.

"Do you need anything, Mama, before I hit the shower?"

"No, baby, you've more than earned your rest. Go take your shower and get some shut eye. Eight o'clock will be here before you know it," Constance warned.

"What happens at eight o'clock?"

"It's third Sunday, boy. You know we always attend church every first and third Sunday. Don't come down here acting brand new. Everyone staying at 331 Oak Street must go to church when the doors swing open. That will never change. Now get some rest," Constance said as she planted a kiss on her son's cheek.

Ryker was too tired to argue, besides, he knew he wouldn't win. Instead, he took a much-needed steaming hot shower and fell across the small double bed that seemed so big to him as a child. Before he could ponder any more thoughts of yester year, sleep took over.

CHAPTER 2

Little had changed about the small, framed white church. The pews were still hard, and the window air conditioning units were still not enough to combat the stifling summer heat. But despite the discomforts, the town's people still filled the church the two Sundays it was open for service. Only in the country did the ministers have to split their pastoral duties between two different churches in two different towns. As Constance chatted away at breakfast, she shared that the church had found a new pastor who was willing to fully commit to Saving Grace Baptist if they could raise the salary to a living wage and install central air. Looking up at the ceiling fans that barely moved and circulated absolutely no air, Ryker thought that the pastor's requests were more than fair.

The choir took their place behind the pulpit and the organist began to play. Constance nudged Ryker in the side and whispered, "This child right here can sing her face off." She nodded towards the young lady that had just lifted the microphone from its stand. She was a stunningly beautiful woman. A mane of reddish-brown curls flowed wildly just past her shoulders. Her five-foot-six-inch frame was toned, yet shapely, soft, and inviting. Her hazel eyes were captivating and when she opened her mouth to sing, it was as if the heavens opened, and a chorus of angels took control of her voice.

"Who is that?" Ryker whispered.

He Won't Go

"That's Lyriq, Bill and Paula James's girl."

Ryker gazed at Lyriq as though she'd cast a spell on him. He listened intently as her voice rose and fell and wrapped itself around every word, making the song more powerful than even its creator thought it could ever be. When she eased off the last note and placed the microphone back in its stand, his heart sank. He wasn't ready for her moment to be over. Ryker relaxed back into the hard pew as the pastor took his place at the altar.

"Let's have another hand clap of praise for Sister Lyriq James." He turned toward the choir stand. "You all are on fire for the Lord this morning."

The congregation clapped and sang out Amens and yes Lords. The pastor passed the microphone to a member of the Courtesy Guild, who welcomed all visitors and read the morning announcements. Once she was done, she passed the mic back to the pastor, who began to give a couple of special announcements of his own.

"Who is this guy and what happened to Reverend Smitty?" Ryker whispered to his mom.

"Reverend Smitty is on vacation, and this is the new pastor I told you about this morning, remember? He's filling in, but we hope to get him permanently. Now pay attention," Constance said as she furrowed her brow and nodded towards the pulpit.

Stacey Covington-Lee

"Now before we move into today's message, church, join me in welcoming back Sister Constance's son, Ryker Adams. This is a hometown boy that went off and made good. He's a big-time engineer out in Irvine, California. Stand up, Ryker, so we can give you a proper welcome."

Embarrassed, Ryker hesitantly stood to his feet and nodded politely at members of the congregation as they stood to applaud his homecoming. After several uncomfortable seconds, he took his seat and was glad to hear the pastor move on with service. As the message was delivered, Ryker had to admit this new guy was actually pretty good. His sermon was both educational and motivating. Nothing like good ole Smitty's sermons that seemed to draw on about his personal experiences, but not much else. Forty-five minutes later, the pastor opened the doors to the church and two visitors felt the calling. The congregation burst into praise as they made their way to the front of the church. Finally, after three more songs from the choir, the deacons took up collection, and the pastor gave the benediction. By the time Ryker made it outside, he was a sweaty mess.

"You ready to head home, Mama?" He asked anxiously. Ryker didn't want to have to greet anyone with sweat stains showing through his dress shirt.

"Just a minute, sweetie. I need to give Sister Paula something."

"Ryker Adams, it's good to see you, brother. Been a long time." The pastor smiled broadly as he approached with an extended hand.

He Won't Go

Ryker took his hand and gave it a firm shake. "Hi there, Reverend Simon, that was a great message you delivered today, but you have to forgive me, you said it's been a long time. We've met before?"

Constance looked on, just as confused as Ryker. She wasn't aware the good reverend had any previous ties to the community.

"I'm not surprised you don't remember, my family moved away when I was in third grade," he chuckled. "You'd probably remember my older brother, Patrick. Everyone called him Pipsqueak."

A light bulb went off for both Ryker and his mom. "Oh man, you're little Jimmie! How have you been? How's your brother? Is he back up this way as well?"

"I've been doing well, finally answered God's call and found my place in the world. Unfortunately, Patrick took a different path and is no longer with us. He moved to Atlanta, got caught up in the drug scene and it cost him his life."

"I'm sorry to hear that, Jimmie. Pipsqueak was a good guy; we had a lot of fun in our younger years."

"Thanks, but enough about that. Are you back down here to stay?" Jimmie quizzed.

"Oh no, just visiting Mom for a couple of weeks and then I've got to get back to work. But I understand you may be taking over the church and overseeing it on a full-time basis."

9

"We sure hope he will," Constance interjected.

"I hope so too. This is a great town full of wonderful people. I'd love to become a permanent part of it."

Before Ryker could respond, he spotted Lyriq as she sauntered in their direction. He hoped his admiration for her beauty wasn't too obvious, but he couldn't take his eyes off her. She was even more beautiful than he initially thought. And apparently, he wasn't the only one that found her attractive. Poor Jimmie was darn near drooling on himself.

"Good afternoon, Ms. Constance, gentlemen," Lyric spoke warmly. "Reverend Simon, that was an awesome message you brought this morning."

"Thank you, Lyriq. I could say the same about that solo you delivered. It was nothing short of soul stirring."

"Thank you," she blushed. "Ms. Constance, my mom wanted me to ask if you remembered to bring that recipe she asked about?"

"Oh yes, baby. I was headed her way, but I'll gladly send it by you. Save me a few steps in these uncomfortable shoes," Constance laughed as she reached into her purse for the index card with the recipe. "Here you go, baby. Tell your mom to call me if she has any questions." It wasn't until Constance looked up that she noticed how Lyriq was coyly smiling at Ryker. "Lyriq, have you met my son, Ryker?"

He Won't Go

"No, but I've heard an awful lot about him," she said as she extended her hand in his direction. "It's a pleasure to finally meet you."

"The pleasure is all mine, and I must agree with the good reverend, you sang beautifully this morning," Ryker complimented as he held on to her hand a little longer than necessary.

Sensing the electricity that was clearly flowing between Ryker and Lyriq, Constance decided to walk off and give them a minute to themselves. Reverend Simon reluctantly followed suit. Everyone could tell the reverend had an attraction to Lyriq, but no one understood why he never acted on it, why he never bothered to ask her out.

"I take it you live here in Allentown?" Ryker quizzed.

"Actually, I live in Macon. I just drive down on Sundays to sing in the choir and visit with my family," Lyriq advised. "And speaking of family, how long will you be here visiting with your mother?"

"I'm here for two weeks, then I'll have to get back out west for work."

"I see."

"Lyriq, please tell me if this is none of my business, but I have to ask. Are you seeing anyone?"

"Wow, you get straight to the point, don't you?"

Stacey Covington-Lee

"No sense in beating around the bush," Ryker said with a shrug of his shoulder.

"I agree and no, I'm not seeing anyone. And you, sir, are you seeing anyone? Is there anyone waiting in the wings, with aspirations of becoming the next Mrs. Ryker Adams?"

Ryker burst into laughter. "The next? Slow down, I've yet to get the first and hopefully only Mrs. Adams."

Constance finished talking to some of the other parishioners and started to ease her way back over to Ryker and Lyriq. The pair caught a glimpse of her and took a moment to look around. Just about everyone had cleared out and Constance was ready to head home as well.

"Lyric, I'm preparing a wonderful dinner this evening. Why don't you stop by on your way back to Macon and join us? I'm baking one of my famous sweet potato pies."

"How can I possibly say no to that?"

"You can't," Constance laughed. "Dinner will be served at five o'clock. See you then."

As soon as they stepped in the house, Ryker made a bee line for the shower. He felt as if someone had poured a barrel of watered-down honey all over him and he had to get it off. Thirty minutes later, he re-emerged feeling fresh and clean, dressed in a crisp white shirt and jeans. He rolled up his sleeves and offered to help with dinner. Not really expecting for Constance to put him to work, he

12

was surprised when she passed him a knife and a large bowl of corn on the cob.

"Mama, what am I supposed to do with this?"

"Boy, I know you haven't forgotten how I taught you to cut the corn from its cob."

"Can't you just open a can of cream corn?"

Constance looked at him as if he'd just said the vilest thing imaginable. Ryker laughed and started cutting the corn. It took him so long that by the time he was done, Constance had prepared everything else, and the corn was the last thing that needed to be cooked before dinner could be served.

"I'm so glad you're a successful engineer and not a cook. The world would starve to death waiting for you to prepare one eatable morsel."

"Very funny," Ryker smirked before jumping at the sound of the doorbell. "I'll get it," he announced as he hopped to his feet and smoothed his shirt.

Over dinner, Ryker learned Lyriq was a twenty-eight-year-old middle school teacher who once had aspirations of becoming a secular singer. In turn, Lyriq learned Ryker was a thirty-two-year-old civil engineer that never wanted to be anything other than what he was. According to Constance, he had always known what he wanted to do and was laser focused on achieving his goals. He'd already made partner at his firm and now had a five-year plan to open his own firm. Lyriq found him so handsome. His thick but toned, six-foot-one inch frame looked as if it were covered in the smoothest dark chocolate known to man. His piercing eyes, perfect teeth, and dimples dripped with sex appeal. Yet, she found him, or rather his ambition, to be very intimidating. She wasn't sure that intellectually she could offer him enough of a challenge. She failed to realize how impressed he was with her talent and creativity. They talked about everything from politics to climate change to entertainment, and even local gossip. She was a total package, but why had she settled for this small-town life?

CHAPTER 3

Ryker hadn't realized how much he'd needed a break from the hustle and bustle of corporate life. The air that was initially stifling was now refreshing. It was still as hot as Texas Pete, but the air was clean, and the occasional breeze felt a little like heaven. His first few days had been spent running errands with his mom. It was as if Constance was afraid he'd leave if she let him out of her sight for more than ten minutes. But Wednesday morning, after she announced she needed to ride over to one of the neighboring towns, Ryker insisted on staying behind and relaxing. After a mid-morning nap, Ryker grabbed a book, climbed in the hammock that swung between two oak trees, and began to read. He couldn't remember the last time he'd held a fictional novel, but this break was the perfect time for him to rejuvenate his love for reading.

He hadn't noticed the Camry when it pulled in front of the house. It wasn't until Jimmie called his name that he realized he wasn't alone.

"Look at you, Ryker, looking like a country boy in that hammock," Jimmie teased.

"Hey man, how are you doing today?"

"I'm doing good. Thought I'd stop by and holler at you since I was passing through."

"I'm glad you did," Ryker said as he hopped down from the hammock. "Come on up here and let's take a seat on the porch. Can I get you something to drink?"

"Don't trouble yourself, man, I'm fine."

"What's been going on with you, Jimmie? How are your folks doing?"

"They're doing well. Mom is retiring from the VA hospital next month, so she and Dad plan to start doing a little traveling. As for me, man, I'm just working and spreading the gospel."

"So, you work outside of the ministry?" Ryker questioned.

"Definitely. You have to remember we're in the country. There are no mega churches raking in mega money down here. I preach a couple of Sundays a month and work full-time as a warehouse manager during the week."

The two continued to share small talk as they watched the occasional car pass by. Eventually the conversation made its way to Lyriq. Ryker couldn't help but wonder why Jimmie, someone people considered successful and a great catch, hadn't tried to date her.

"To be honest with you, Ryker, I'm very serious about my calling. I want to date and ultimately marry a woman who is going to help me build something special for the kingdom of God. I want someone who's not only beautiful, but spiritual, and untouched by some of the harsher aspects of life."

He Won't Go

Ryker looked completely baffled. "Wouldn't someone who's experienced some challenges and come out on the other side have a greater testimony of God's goodness? Wouldn't their difficulties make them more relatable?"

"You make an excellent point and ordinarily I'd say yes. But after watching Pipsqueak's struggle with drugs, I can't bring myself to deal with anyone who has had any type of involvement. My heart can't take watching another person lose their soul to the demon of drugs."

A look of shock painted itself across Ryker's face. "Are you telling me that Lyriq is a drug addict?"

"I can't really speak for her and what labels she's attached to herself, but she did go through a period where she was heavily into drugs. Losing her banking career was the reality check that it took for her to seek help."

"Oh, so she hasn't always been a teacher?"

"Nah, she got her certification after a three-month stint in rehab. Her family blamed her move to Atlanta for the drug use, but truth be told, just as many addicts are bred down here as in the city. Gangs and pushers have infiltrated these little towns."

"Wow, I never would've imagined anything like that. Gangs in South Georgia seems so farfetched. But tell me, how long ago did she have this drug issue?"

Jimmie tilted his head and looked at Ryker suspiciously. "You seem to have a lot of interest in Lyriq."

"I'm just curious, man. I never would've imagined someone like her would have a drug problem," Ryker confessed.

"Had, past tense. She's been clean for about five years now."

"Then why are you still holding it against her?" Ryker continued to question.

"Don't get me wrong, Lyriq is a beautiful, smart woman and I certainly don't mean to hold her past against her. I know God can change anyone, but what I witnessed with my brother was enough to deter me from dealing with anyone who has firsthand knowledge of that life. Recovering addicts slip back into their addiction every day. I'm simply not willing to deal with that possibility."

"I hear you, Jimmie. It's awfully hard losing a loved one the way you lost Pipsqueak."

Silence fell between the two old friends as they both seemed to get lost in their own thoughts. Finally, Jimmie stood to his feet and announced his need to get on down the road. Ryker stood and the two shared a brotherly handshake and hug. After making Ryker promise to attend church again before his return to California, Jimmie jumped in his car and took off.

Ryker returned to the hammock and tried to continue reading his book, but he couldn't get thoughts of Lyriq out of his head.

He Won't Go

"Jimmie's probably right, addicts slip all the time," he mumbled to himself. "And she's probably not even worth the trouble."

An hour later, Ryker felt someone gently shaking his shoulder. He slowly opened his eyes and looked up into the face of an angel. He quickly sat up and almost fell out of the hammock.

"Be careful," Lyriq giggled. "I'm sorry for waking you, but I was headed to pick something up from my mom's house and didn't want to pass by without saying hello.

"I'm so glad you did," Ryker smiled as he stood to his feet. "Why don't we head in the house? It's cool and comfortable in there." He offered his hand and was pleased when she took it and walked with him in the house. "Please have a seat, make yourself at home. I'll be back in just a minute."

He dashed off to the bathroom where he filled his mouth with Scope. After several seconds of swishing, Ryker checked himself in the mirror and brushed his hair. He felt like a schoolboy that had just won a date with a cheerleader. He couldn't help but laugh at himself as he returned to the front of the house.

"What's so funny?"

"Oh nothing, just laughing at my goofy self. Would you like something to drink?"

"Iced tea would be nice," Lyriq smiled with a tilt of her head.

"The staple of every southern home. Come on in the kitchen and I'll get you a glass. I'm a little hungry myself. Care to join me for a snack?"

Lyriq stood to her feet and followed Ryker through the small, but nicely appointed home. "No thanks, the tea will be fine." She stopped in front of a shelf full of pictures. Smiling at one in particular, she asked, "How old were you here?"

"Geez, I was eight or nine. Thought I was cool, but as you can see, I was mistaken."

The pair continued their short journey to the kitchen where they sat and talked for almost two hours. They hadn't even realized how time had gotten away until Constance returned home. She tried to convince Lyriq to stay and join them for dinner, but Lyriq politely declined. She had to get to her mom's house and then make her way home and grade papers. Always the gentleman, Ryker walked her out to her car as Constance stood with a look of uncertainty etched across her face. A few minutes later, Ryker returned with a smile stuck to his lips.

"She's a great girl, isn't she?"

"Yes, she is," Constance admitted. She then turned her back and mumbled, "But she's the one thing I'm glad you'll be leaving behind when you return to California."

CHAPTER 4

To Constance's disappointment, almost every waking minute of Ryker's last week at home had been spent with Lyriq. She was glad her son was enjoying his time back in the south, but a little jealous more wasn't spent with her and concerned he'd become so enamored with that woman. It's not that Constance thought Lyriq was a bad person, but her past drug addiction gave Constance reason for pause. Yes, Lyriq had successfully completed treatment and yes, she'd re-established a successful career, but could she be trusted to stay clean for the rest of her life? Constance shook the thoughts away as she continued to fold her laundry. She decided thinking about it was a waste of time because Ryker was leaving in two days and Lyriq would still be in Macon. The distance would kill any hope of a real relationship.

The clock struck midnight and Constance had grown tired of waiting for her son to return home. She'd hoped to spend a little time talking with him before bed, but clearly, he had other plans. She decided to fix a cup of tea and finish watching her Lifetime movie in bed. While she was addicted to the predictable storylines and psycho characters, she had a tendency to always fall asleep before the movie could conclude. She figured tonight would be no exception. Constance sat her cup of tea on the nightstand and got on her knees to say her nightly prayers. She prayed God would bring her son safely home, that when he returned to California, Lyriq would only be a fond memory, and he'd eventually find a woman that deserved to hold his heart.

~~~

Ryker and Lyriq had taken the quick two-hour ride to Atlanta to enjoy a great meal and Jazz concert in the park. They laughed, danced, and as usual, shared great conversation. Ryker had never found it so easy to be with a woman. He felt comfortable to be himself and was secure in the fact that she wasn't looking to get anything from him. She simply enjoyed his company as much as he enjoyed hers. As they drove back home, Lyriq held on as long as she could, but forty minutes in she'd fallen fast asleep. Ryker chuckled as the low buzz of her snoring mixed with the music that played softly through the speakers.

An hour later, Ryker pulled into Lyriq's driveway, killed the ignition to the car, and gently roused her from her slumber.

"Wake up, beautiful," he said softly as he gently stroked the side of her face. "Let's get you inside so you can sleep comfortably."

Lyriq smiled as she watched him walk around to her side of the car. He opened the door, held out his hand, and escorted her to the front door. She was not ready for this to end, feeling as though she'd just found her soul mate, she wasn't ready to see him leave town. She didn't want him to drop out of her life just as quickly as he'd dropped in. She held his hand tightly and wished on the stars above that he'd remain in her life.

"I guess this is it, sweetness. Although I'm dedicating tomorrow to my mom, I promise to swing through here and see you again before I head to the airport in Atlanta."

"I'm going to hold you to that promise."

"Nothing short of death will make me break it," he whispered as he took her face in his hands and kissed her lovingly.

Taking the keys from her hand, Ryker unlocked the door, waited for her to cross the threshold, and turned to leave. But the magnetic pull between the two wouldn't let him go. He turned around and ran back to the door before she could close it. He pushed his way in the house and took her in his arms. This time the kiss wasn't sweet, it was one of pure, unbridled passion. It took every ounce of strength he had not to rip the clothes from her body and take her right there on the floor. But with him leaving in two days, that wouldn't be fair to either of them. Finally pulling himself away, he gave her one last peck on the forehead, turned and left.

Lyriq stood in her doorway and watched until he drove out of sight. She closed the door and slid down to the floor. Tears rolled down her face and her emotions were all over the place. How could she have fallen so fast and hard for someone she knew was a temporary fixture in her life? She knew once Ryker left, her life would return to its mundane existence and no matter what man approached her, regardless of what he had to offer, he'd never compare to Ryker.

"Lord, how am I supposed to let this man go? Why did you even bring him into my life if he couldn't stay?" She questioned, but no answers came. Was this her punishment for going astray and living an unrighteous life? She thought she'd made amends by going to treatment, getting clean, confessing her sins, and asking forgiveness, but clearly none of that was enough. Like her mother always said, you're forgiven, but you still have to be punished. Lyriq took a deep breath and pulled herself up from the floor. She headed to the bathroom and let her tears mix with the steaming hot water from the shower. By the time she turned the water off, she'd purged her soul and accepted her punishment. Ryker would never be hers.

~~~

The smell of bacon drew Ryker out of his slumber. He rubbed his eyes, stretched and smiled as he replayed his evening with Lyriq. But the smile faded as the realization of leaving her sank in. He didn't know how he'd do it, but one thing was for sure, he had to get back to his job and life in California. His dream of starting his own firm would not become a reality if he didn't get back and bring it to fruition. He jumped up, showered, and joined his mom in the kitchen.

"It smells amazing in here. Did you make your homemade biscuits?" Ryker asked as he popped a piece of bacon in his mouth.

He Won't Go

"Boy, what have I told you about snatching food? And yes, they're in the oven. I thought after two weeks, you'd be tired of those things."

"Seriously? You know I'll never tire of those biscuits. They're like eating a piece of heaven. How much longer before they're ready?"

Constance slipped on an oven mitt, opened the warmer, and pulled out a baking sheet full of honey butter biscuits. She loaded her son's plate up with thick cut bacon, cheese grits, scrambled eggs, and biscuits. She loved seeing him eat so hardily.

"I tried waiting up for you last night, but by the time midnight rolled around, I gave up the ghost and went to bed. I thought you'd be in fairly early since Lyriq had to be at work this morning. Students can't learn from a sleepy teacher."

"She was fine, Ma. We went up to Atlanta for a while and she got to sleep in the car on the way back. Besides, today ends the school year and they're not doing anything but playing all day."

"I see. Well, I'm glad you two got a chance to enjoy yourselves before you head back to California. Nothing like a little summer fling to relax you before getting back to the grind of work."

"I don't know, this thing between Lyriq and me doesn't feel like it should just be a fling. She feels like forever," Ryker confessed to his mother's horror.

Stacey Covington-Lee

Constance poured them more coffee and tried to speak as kindly as she could. "Baby, she is not your forever. Lyriq is a lovely young woman, but she's also a troubled one. Your life is on the fast track, and you don't need to have it derailed by her. This was a fling and now it's time for you to get back to real life."

"I know about her troubles, Ma. I also know she has overcome them, turned her life over to God, and is living righteously. Now if God can forgive and forget, why can't you?"

Constance drew in a deep breath. Her son's words stung a little, but she only had his best interest at heart. "Sweetheart, there was nothing for me to forgive. She never wronged me, and I remember her past transgressions because I'm human. And because she's human, there is always the chance of slipping back into that addiction. That's just not something I want you to invite into your life."

Ryker looked at his mom but decided against any further conversation pertaining to Lyriq. Instead, he made the day extra special for his mom. They shopped as if the stores were going out of business, visited other family and friends, and shared lots of laughter. For Constance, the day was all she could've hoped for. She didn't think it could get any better, but little did she know her son had a beautiful surprise waiting at the church.

"Baby, why are we here at the church? Service is tomorrow."

He Won't Go

"Yeah, but I have to leave so early I'm going to miss it. So, I asked Jimmie and the board members to meet us here."

"For what?" Constance quizzed.

"Just get out the car, Mama. We don't want to keep the folks waiting."

Ryker knew how much his mom wanted for Jimmie to be their full-time pastor. She wanted service every Sunday, not just twice a month. With that thought in mind, he stood before the pastor, the board, and his mom and presented them with a one hundred-thousand-dollar donation. That was more than enough to have central air installed, make a couple of other upgrades to the church, and have plenty left over to help towards Jimmie's pay increase.

"All I ask in return is that you dedicate my mom's favorite pew to her, by affixing a small plaque to it with her name engraved on it."

Jimmie walked over to Ryker and gave him a brotherly hug. "I don't know how to thank you for this. It's more than any of us could've ever hoped for."

Constance rocked back and forth as tears of pride ran down her cheeks. Jimmie and the board members thanked him again and assured him the pew dedication would take place on the next first Sunday. Satisfied he'd made his mother happy, he took her by the hand, and they left for home. The remainder of the evening was filled with conversation, peach cobbler, and prayer.

Stacey Covington-Lee

The driver arrived at Constance's house at eight a.m., loaded Ryker's bags, and waited patiently while he and his mom said their goodbyes. The next stop was Lyriq's place. Ryker went inside and held the woman who'd captured his heart while silent tears fell from her eyes. They kissed and then he was gone.

CHAPTER 5

To say he was distracted was a major understatement. Ryker had tried to throw himself back into his work, but it seemed he couldn't concentrate on anything other than how much he wished he could see Lyriq. She seemed to be his first and last thought of each day. They talked on the phone daily, but it wasn't the same. He wanted her mind, body and soul, not just her long-distance conversation. He stood looking out of his office window replaying their time together when he heard a baritone voice speak to him.

"Man, just send for her."

Ryker turned to see his friend, Kane, standing in the doorway of his office. The night he got back to Irvine, the two of them had gone out for drinks and Ryker told Kane all about the beautiful Lyriq. Kane listened intently as it became increasingly evident that his boy had gone to the country and fallen in love. Ryker figured like everyone else, Kane would have concerns because of Lyriq's past, but then Kane reminded him of his own past with drugs.

"Man, I'm ten years clean and sober. Once a user doesn't mean always a user," Kane reminded him. That conversation was days ago, yet Ryker was still being less than productive. It was evident his thoughts were back in Georgia.

"I'm sorry, what did you say?"

"I said just send for her. Send that Lyriq girl a round-trip ticket to come visit. You said that school was out for summer down there, so she's likely free as a bird. Please, send for her so we can get some work out of you."

It's not like Ryker hadn't thought of that a million times, he just didn't know how receptive Lyriq would be to the idea. But he decided to take a leap of faith. That evening he went online and purchased a round trip ticket with an open return date. He had the tickets emailed to Lyriq and then called her for their nightly chat.

"Babe, do me a favor and check your email."

Lyriq did as he asked and found it impossible to contain her joy. When she saw the airline tickets, she squealed like a schoolgirl and danced around the room as if she'd caught the Holy Ghost.

"Does that mean you'll come?" Ryker asked, although he knew the answer.

"Just tell me when you want me there."

"I booked it for this Thursday. Does that give you enough time to prepare?"

"You'd better know it," Lyriq replied gleefully. "I'm going to be the first one in the terminal Thursday morning, anxiously waiting to get to you."

By the next morning, Ryker seemed to have magically returned to his focused, productive self. He worked with a renewed purpose and dedication that did not go unnoticed by his peers. When Ryker was on point, he expected the same from everyone around him. It's how he helped to keep the firm ranked among the top ten in the country.

"Let me guess, she agreed to come," Kane smiled as he stepped into Ryker's office.

"How did you know?"

"Man, you're buzzing around here like a hyper little beaver and got the office staff jumping too. I just hope your energy remains this high once little Miss Lyriq arrives."

"No need to worry about that," Ryker assured him. "Having her with me will not be a distraction, but rather a motivator. Getting in and getting things done will set all my evenings free so I can enjoy my time with her. Trust me, there will be no slacking."

"That's good to hear, because the representatives from Armetron will be arriving from Canada next week, and our presentation has got to be on point. They're ready to invest big money in their U.S. facility and if we're awarded the contract, it'll be a financial windfall for us all."

Ryker whipped open some drawings he'd been working on, along with detailed descriptions of what he had in mind for the facility. "Despite my distractions, I actually got a decent amount of preliminary work done. I just need to review it with you and the rest of the team to ensure we all share the same vision."

31

"These look great," Kane nodded. "I'll book a conference room this afternoon, make sure we're all on the same page, and then you can move full steam ahead."

The afternoon meeting went just as Ryker had hoped. The team made a few tweaks to his drawings and suggested additional features to be added to the facility. This was to be one of the most technologically advanced structures in the country. With Ryker leading the charge, it could make the goal of starting his own firm a reality much sooner than he'd anticipated.

Once the meeting adjourned, Ryker returned to his office to find three urgent messages from Constance. Anxious to make sure everything was alright, he pulled out his cell and dialed her number.

"Mom, what's going on, is everything okay?"

"I ran into Lyriq's mother, and she told me that you'd sent for that child. Is it true, is she flying out there tomorrow?"

"Actually, she is flying out Thursday. Just two more days and I'll be blessed with her presence," Ryker gushed.

"Do you really consider that a blessing, son? She has a past, the kind of past you have no experience with, and one I never want you to be a part of. Don't get me wrong, she's nice enough, but you need to find someone without that type of baggage."

"Mama, listen to yourself. You're a faithful, God fearing, and supposedly forgiving woman. Why can't you let her past go?"

He Won't Go

"I fear she'll return to her drug abusing past. I don't mean to hold it against her, but I don't want my son dragged into it."

"She's not dragging me anywhere, Mama. And for the record, I do believe her being here will be a blessing. I'm choosing to ignore all of your negativity and focus on loving her with the love of The Lord, the way you taught me."

"That's beautiful, baby, but you don't have to be in a relationship with her to love her with the love of The Lord. She doesn't need to visit you for that," Constance continued to protest.

"Well Mama, I'm a grown man, being with her is what I want. She makes me happy."

"Baby, just listen to me---"

"I love you, Mama," Ryker interrupted. "But I won't listen to any more of this. I've got to get back to work. I love you and will chat with you later."

He didn't wait to hear his mother say goodbye, he knew instead she'd only continue to protest, so he disconnected the call. Ryker knew no matter who he dated, his mother wouldn't think they were good enough. Of course, he wanted his mom to be happy for him, but he wasn't willing to wait the rest of his life for her approval.

CHAPTER 6

Lyriq felt like a super star as she rounded the corner to baggage claim and spotted a driver dressed in a black suit and tie, holding a sign with her name on it. A broad smile crossed her face as she approached him and introduced herself. He gathered her bags and escorted her to the waiting town car.

"Miss James, we should arrive at Mr. Adams's office within the hour," the driver advised as they pulled away from the curb.

"Thank you and please, call me Lyriq."

After hitting a wall of traffic, Lyriq decided to put in her ear buds and finish listening to the audio book she'd started on the plane. She was so anxious to get to Ryker and the story was a great distraction to keep her from screaming about the traffic delaying their reunion. Finally, after an hour and a half ride, they pulled up to a beautiful, six-story glass building and Ryker was standing outside to greet her. Clearly, the driver had called him as they were approaching. Lyriq didn't wait for the driver to open her door. As soon as the car stopped, she jumped out and threw her arms around Ryker. Their embrace was tight and full of warmth.

"I'm so glad to have you here," Ryker whispered in her ear.

"I'm glad to be here," she whispered back as she planted a gentle kiss on his cheek.

He Won't Go

The driver was kind enough to haul Lyriq's bags up to Ryker's office and was tipped very generously for his troubles. Ryker took the time to proudly introduce Lyriq to his co-workers as they made their way up to his office. Finally, behind closed doors, Ryker pulled her into his arms again, this time kissing her with all the passion he'd held back earlier. Though they'd shared kisses before, they were mostly polite, sweet kisses and that's what Ryker had intended this time, but his emotions wouldn't let him hold back. Just as he was going in for yet another kiss, there was a knock at the door.

"Come in," Ryker called out as he wiped Lyriq's lipstick from his mouth.

"This must be your lady love, Lyriq," Kane smiled as he glided into the office. He reached for her hand and gave it a firm yet gentle shake. "My friend here said you were beautiful, but that doesn't do you justice. You are stunning."

Ryker stood beside them shaking his head. Kane was a true Dapper Don. He was smooth as silk and the ladies swooned in his presence. But to see Lyriq politely smile, exchange pleasantries, and pull her hand away as if he were a little slimy both tickled and pleased Ryker. It was clear the only man in the room she was interested in was him.

"Dude, that smooth talk of yours doesn't work on everyone," Ryker teased.

"I can accept that. Besides, there's nothing like a loyal woman and little Miss Lyriq here seems to be just that. Welcome to Irvine, Lyriq. All joking aside, it is a pleasure to meet you and I hope the two of you will join my lady friend and I for dinner tomorrow night, my treat of course."

"How generous of you," Lyriq smiled. "Will it be okay if we let you know a little later on?"

"Of course, Ryker knows where to find me. You two carry on with your reunion and Ryker, don't keep her hanging around this boring place too long."

Three hours later, the couple finally departed the office building. Ryker apologized emphatically as he explained the importance of the project he was working on. Lyriq lovingly caressed his face as they drove away. She assured him she was fine and didn't want to distract him from his work. She was more than happy to sight-see alone by day and enjoy his company by night. She wanted to be a great support, not a distraction and certainly not a burden.

As Ryker pulled up to his condominium complex, Lyriq couldn't help gawking in awe. While Atlanta had many gorgeous housing developments, lofts, and condos, none struck her the way his did. The building was an angular structure, each unit had a massive terrace, and the grounds were immaculate. The doorman was friendly and fell over himself to assist Ryker with her bags. Just when she thought it couldn't get any better, Ryker unlocked his door and she stepped into real estate paradise. The open floor plan had been professionally decorated and could have easily been featured in Architectural Digest. Impressed was not a sufficient enough word to describe Lyriq's reaction. She eased over to the floor to ceiling windows that separated her from the terrace. Ryker walked up behind her, unlocked the glass door, wrapped his arms around her waist, and walked her outside. He pointed out various landmarks while snuggling her from behind. As much as she wanted to pay attention, his scent, the feel of his arms, and his low seductive voice made it almost impossible. Lyriq found herself turning around to face Ryker. She got lost in his eyes and without a second thought, she pressed her lips to his and kissed him passionately. As the intensity grew, she felt herself being pushed away.

"Why don't we step inside, let me show you the rest of the place?" Ryker took her by the hand and escorted her back into the condo. He gave her the grand tour, finally showing her to the guest room she'd be occupying during her visit. He placed her bags in the room and asked if the space would be sufficient. Lyriq looked around at the beautifully appointed room with its king-sized bed, flat screen television, and super-sized window that overlooked the city. The en-suite bath with its walk-in shower and footed bath were so inviting. The plush robe, thick towels, and scented candles added to the attractiveness of the room. And the blue Tiffany box that rested on the nightstand was impossible to ignore.

Stacey Covington-Lee

"Everything is gorgeous, Ryker. This is more than I expected and far more than I'll ever need. Thank you so much for flying me out and welcoming me into your home."

"No need to thank me, I did this for me. I would've done just about anything to spend time with you," he confessed as he leaned over and planted the sweetest kiss on her forehead. "Now, how about we freshen up and head out to dinner?"

"Sounds good to me, I'm starving."

"Do me a favor first," Ryker asked. "Open that box," he said, pointing to the Tiffany box. "I think it will be the perfect accessory to whatever you wear to dinner tonight."

Lyriq opened the box and saw a magnificent diamond bangle. Her eyes welled up as Ryker placed the bracelet on her arm. No one had ever shown her such kindness. No man had ever cared enough to buy her beautiful gifts, instead, they'd wanted to buy her.

The Hobbit restaurant was an upscale eatery that housed an extensive wine cellar and menu options so delectable it made choosing a meal a chore. Lyriq finally settled on the filet mignon with truffle sauce while Ryker enjoyed his favorite, beef wellington. The pair shared their food as well as great conversation. Lyriq filled him in on the latest country gossip while Ryker mapped out some of the activities he had in store for them. And while Ryker was thoroughly enjoying himself, he yearned for deeper conversation. He wanted to discuss her past, her fears, and hopes for the future. He

38

wanted to know all there was to know about Lyriq but realized when he opened the door to that kind of deep dialog, he'd be obligated to share everything about himself as well.

It was late when they returned, and Ryker knew Lyriq was exhausted. They shared gentle kisses and polite hugs before Ryker bid her a goodnight. He went to his room and closed the door behind him. Lyriq stood for a moment longer, a little baffled by his behavior, before entering her room and closing the door. She placed the stopper in the tub and turned on the faucet. Steam began to rise from the bath as she disrobed. Carefully, she slid into the sultry waters until her body rested comfortably on the bottom of the tub. As she soaked, she wondered if the rest of her stay would be like today, wonderful but lacking passion. What would it take to make herself more desirable to Ryker? What would make him stop keeping her at arm's length?

CHAPTER 7

"You have no idea how much I wish I could take the day off and spend it with you, but this deal we're trying to close dictates that I go in," Ryker explained.

"I totally understand. I'll be here waiting when you get in. We'll enjoy time together then. Oh, are we going to dinner with your friends?"

"If you're up for it, I'd love to."

"I'm up for anything, Mr. Adams," Lyriq teased.

"Don't play with me, woman," he smirked. "Look, I don't want you stuck in the house all day, so I've arranged for a driver to pick you up around noon. There's some decent shopping here if you're interested, or they can take you wherever you like. I should be back by five at the latest." Ryker planted a kiss on her forehead as he handed her a house key. One more kiss and he was out the door.

Lyriq walked to the terrace door and stepped outside. She drank in the morning sun and patiently waited to see Ryker's car exit the parking garage. She smiled as she thought about a future with Ryker. She imagined herself with a gorgeous wedding ring on her finger and a precious baby in her belly. She knew she was getting way ahead of herself, but no one had ever made her feel as special or as wanted as he had. But she was still aware of a weird distance between them, one she'd have to figure out how to conquer.

As she stepped back into the house, temptation gripped Lyriq like a golfer holding his nine iron. She wanted to take off to Ryker's bedroom and snoop through his personal belongings. Maybe there was some deep dark secret he was hiding, or something that would explain why she wasn't invited to stay in there with him as opposed to the guest room. However, her common sense and high level of respect kicked in and she knew she couldn't, in good conscience, invade his privacy. Instead, she headed to her room, freshened up, and dressed for the day. She remembered seeing a cute little café on the corner and decided to walk over for coffee. Lyriq was greeted warmly by the staff and ushered to a cozy little booth where she perused the menu.

"Good morning, sweetheart. What can I get you to drink?" The motherly looking waitress asked.

"Good morning. May I please have a hot caramel latte?"

"Coming right up," the waitress smiled as she turned, and her large hips sashayed across the room to retrieve Lyriq's coffee.

Looking around, Lyriq noticed the café was mostly filled with women either holding toddlers, or with babies in strollers. She couldn't tell if they were the mothers or the nannies. There were a couple of guys huddled at a table in the corner. The conversation looked intense, was it a business meeting or a lover's quarrel? Then one of the men reached across the small table and took the other's hand and his facial expression softened. *A lover's quarrel made good* she thought.

"Here you are, sweetie, an extra sweet caramel latte."

"I didn't ask for it extra sweet," Lyriq half-heartedly protested.

"Do you want me to take it back and bring a regular one?"

"I didn't say all that," Lyriq smiled as she pulled the steaming hot cup closer to her.

"Now that that's settled, what can I get you to eat?"

"May I have the French toast please?"

"Yes, you may, and I'll bring you a side of eggs. You need the protein to balance the meal."

"Um, oh, okay… Thank you," Lyriq stuttered. She glanced around to see if her mother was there giving the waitress instructions. Five minutes later, the waitress returned with her food. They exchanged a few more pleasantries before the lady left to wait on another table. Lyriq enjoyed her meal, scrolled through her social media pages, and called her mom for a brief chat before returning to the condo. She wasn't inside five minutes before the doorbell rang. Through the peephole she saw a young woman sporting a black suit and driver's cap. "Must be my ride," she mumbled as she opened the door.

He Won't Go

"Good afternoon, Miss. James, my name is Bailey and I'm your driver for the afternoon. Are you ready to leave or would you like for me to wait for you downstairs?"

"Hello, Bailey, please call me Lyriq and I'll be ready shortly. I just need to change purses, but please have a seat. You're welcome to wait here."

"Thank you, ma'am."

"Girl, stop. I told you, call me Lyriq. We've got to be about the same age, so that ma'am stuff is a no go," Lyriq chuckled.

With a laugh and a slight nod, Bailey took a seat and crossed her legs. She never removed her cap, but Lyriq could see the silky straight, honey blonde hair tucked underneath it. Her makeup was flawless, her suite was fitted, and she sported a pair of stilettos. Bailey had to be the most fashionable driver Lyric had ever encountered. After disappearing to her bedroom for about five minutes, Lyriq re-emerged, and the ladies headed out.

Bailey opened the back door of the black town car for Lyriq. Once she was situated, Bailey took her seat behind the wheel. "Where would you like to go, Lyriq?"

"Take me to the best shopping mall in town."

"You've got it. It should only take us fifteen minutes or so to arrive at the Spectrum Center. The shopping is pretty decent, but it's an entertaining place. If the shopping doesn't suit your fancy, we'll move on to a couple of other malls."

43

"Sounds good. So, Bailey, I'm a little curious. Do you always dress in high heels when you drive?"

"Absolutely not. I was supposed to have a meeting earlier today, but in my rush out the door, I forgot to grab my flats." Bailey explained.

"Well hopefully, it was a good, productive meeting."

"Nope, it got cancelled just ten minutes before it was scheduled to start. I was too lazy to drive back home, so instead I grabbed a bite to eat and here I am."

As the day went on, the two ladies shared more about themselves with one another. They seemed to have little in common, but still clicked really well. There was a mutual respect and comfort level they had with each other. Lyriq talked Bailey into abandoning her car and shopping with her. Bailey purchased a pair of flats and the two struck out, moving from store to store, laughing and shopping. When it was time to head back, Lyriq jumped in the front passenger seat so they could continue to interact as friends and not as driver and customer. Finally, back at the condo, the pair exchanged phone numbers and said their goodbyes.

~~~

"Lyriq, I'm so sorry I got delayed. We have seven o'clock reservations, but if you'd like to bail on them, I totally understand," Ryker bellowed as he rushed through the door. Before he could make his way further into the condo, he was stopped in his tracks by a vision of beauty. Lyriq rounded the corner dressed as if she was straight off the pages of a fashion magazine. From head to toe, she was flawless.

"You look incredible."

"Why thank you, Mr. Adams. Since you were running late, I didn't want to be responsible for delaying us any further. So, whenever you're ready, I'm ready."

Ryker didn't immediately respond. Instead, he drank in the beauty of her curls pulled up into a loose, soft bun, the off the shoulder dress that hugged her curves but didn't overly sexualize her, and the six-inch strappy stilettos that made her calf muscles pop. He wanted more than anything to sweep her off her feet and make passionate, ravenous love to her. He slowly shook his head, tying to remove the thought from it. He walked over and wrapped her in a warm embrace. Inhaling her scent, Ryker found himself gently kissing her neck, then taking her face in his hands and kissing her lustfully. It took every ounce of strength he had to pull himself away.

"I want you so badly right now," he whispered. "But we shouldn't be late. Let me clean up real quick and we'll head out." He planted one more quick kiss on her lips and then disappeared into his room.

Lyriq walked over to the terrace, trying to calm the butterflies in her stomach. Would tonight be the night he let down his guard and allow nature to take its course? Lyriq closed her eyes and said a little prayer. *Father, I know that what I'm asking is actually a sin, but we know I am not perfect. We all sin and fall short of Your glory. Father, either strengthen me and remove these desires, or forgive me for acting on them. Forgive me for wanting this man so badly. "*

It wasn't long before Lyriq felt a strong arm wrap itself around her waist. Ryker kissed her neck and whispered, "Ready to go, sexy?"

"With you? Always."

The pair made the thirty-minute journey to the restaurant. The hostess led them to the lounge area where Kane and his date, Mona, were waiting for their arrival. After a brief introduction, the hostess returned to escort the foursome to their table. As the waiter took their drink orders, Lyriq found herself giving Mona the once-over. She was tall for a woman, at least five foot nine and a perfect size six. Her big, round eyes and hazelnut complexion could've made her a perfect model for the *Victoria's Secret* catalog. In sharp contrast, her voice reminded Lyriq of a sixty-year-old who'd smoked half her life.

As the men chatted about work, Lyriq attempted to engage Mona in conversation. A simple question about her occupation had turned into her giving a decertation about the fundamentals of candle making. She droned on for what seemed like forever and Lyriq could only hope she wouldn't be quizzed on what the woman was babbling about. The waiter approached with drinks and Lyriq hoped that a cocktail would occupy Mona's mouth and distract her from further conversation, but no such luck.

He Won't Go

"Lyriq, do you have a preference in which kind of candles you burn? You know, wax or soy?" Mona quizzed.

Lyriq reached under the table and caressed Ryker's thigh as she replied with a sly grin, "I like the ones that melt down into massage oil."

"Ooh, sounds like someone has naughty plans for the night," Mona joked, not realizing how much Lyriq wanted her statement to be true. Making naughty plans wasn't the issue but getting Ryker to participate might prove to be a little troublesome.

The evening went on with more mindless chatter and thankfully, a delicious meal. The food made Mona's ramblings a little more tolerable. But once the food was gone and their tongues were tired, the couples bid each other a good night.

"Mona is quite talkative, isn't she?" Ryker chuckled as he slid into the driver's seat.

"Oh, my goodness, Ryker, I thought that woman would never shut up. I mean, she seems nice enough, but it was like someone put batteries in her mouth and set her on go."

"Something tells me Kane feels the same way about her. Clearly, he tolerates her for other reasons. But enough about them, let's go listen to a little Jazz under the stars."

"That sounds lovely," Lyriq replied, although she preferred to go back to his place so they could get closer.

Stacey Covington-Lee

As if reading her mind, Ryker turned the car around and headed home. "Better yet, let's head home and enjoy one another." He glanced at Lyriq and the smile that crossed her face warmed his heart.

They held hands and listened to music as Ryker sped down the freeway towards the exit. Thirty minutes later, they were back at the condo. Lyriq suggested they each go change into something more comfortable and meet back on the sofa. As she closed the door to her bedroom, Ryker prepared an ice bucket with a bottle of sparkling cider and grabbed a couple of wine glasses. He placed the items on the small table that sat between two lounge chairs on his terrace. After turning on some soft Jazz, he quickly fled to his room to change into a pair of drawstring bottoms and a t-shirt. When he returned to the terrace, Lyriq was already there relaxing in a slinky negligee. One look at her and he knew it would take every ounce of strength he had to not jump her sexy bones.

CHAPTER 8

The evening hadn't gone as Lyriq had hoped. Yes, they had a beautiful time together. The music, the stars, and the two of them sharing one lounge chair. She'd snuggled close to Ryker and caressed his chest while he engaged in small talk, an obvious ploy to try to keep from being intimate. But it seemed he couldn't avoid it completely. Despite his best efforts, he caved to the intense feelings of lust. It wasn't long before they were sharing passionate, breathless kisses. He'd pulled her on top of him and she could feel the strength of his manhood as he began to caress her body. But just as quickly as it began, he brought it to a screeching halt.

Holding her around her waist, he sat up in the chair and looked her square in the eye. "I have never fallen for a woman the way I am falling for you. Not only do I want to make love to you, but I want to love you, mind, body, and soul. To have your body isn't enough for me, I want all of you, but I've got to know more about you. I want to hear about your struggles, why you've chosen the life you have, and what you want for your future." He gently stroked her face. "Please tell me your greatest fear?"

Silent tears spilled from Lyriq's eyes. No one had cared enough to want to know everything about her. They would've gladly taken her body, used her love until they'd used it up and walked away. She was overwhelmed with emotion. In that moment, she decided to share with him what she'd never shared with any man.

"My greatest fear is being tempted with drugs and falling back into that lifestyle. It's a horrible place to be and I don't ever want to go there again."

He kissed her tears and snuggled her close. "Do you mind telling me how you got involved with drugs in the first place?"

The memory of it shook Lyriq to her core. Too ashamed to tell the truth with Ryker looking her directly in the face, she tried to turn her back to him, but he wouldn't allow it.

"Nothing you say to me will change my opinion of you, or how I feel about you. Please look at me and speak your truth."

She kissed him sweetly and began. "You know how much I love to sing. Once upon a time I aspired to sing professionally, so after work I started performing at open mic nights around Atlanta. I thought I'd caught my big break when a music producer heard me sing one night and offered to produce my first single. I really thought he was on my side. We worked together for a few weeks, finding the perfect song and all. We'd been working so hard; we were tired, and he said he needed to relax a bit. He pulled out a joint and started smoking. He offered me a pull and I thought why not, it's just weed. I had no idea that it was laced with cocaine. I was so high that I had no control over my own body, I had no strength to fight, and he knew it." Lyriq sniffed and wiped tears. "He assaulted me that night and as hurt as I was, I was back the next night. Not for the music, but for the coke. That one pull was all it took to get me hooked."

The way Lyriq's body shook with tears broke Ryker's heart. He pulled her even closer as if trying to transfer her hurt and shame onto himself. "It's okay, babe, I'm right here and I've got you. I'll always have you," he lovingly reassured.

His comforting arms and reassuring words made her feel safe, made her feel as if he'd protect her from the world, but that was last night. As she looked around the condo, she wondered where he'd snuck off to. Was he somewhere trying to figure out how to rid himself of the addict inhabiting his home? Lyriq sighed deeply as she pushed herself up from the chair at the kitchen table. Her coffee cup was empty, and she decided to go and start packing. Apparently, her truth was too much for Ryker to handle. She was pulling her suitcase from the closet when she heard Ryker come through the front door, belting her name.

"Hey, is everything okay?" Lyriq asked as she stepped from the bedroom.

"Everything will be great once you throw a couple things in an overnight bag. We're going to take a trip. Can you be ready in thirty minutes? Kane and that annoying Mona are going to meet us at the airport within the hour."

"Thirty minutes! Oh gracious, let me jump in the shower and make myself look decent," Lyriq dashed back into the room feeling thankful. It didn't matter where he wanted to go, the fact that he still wanted her with him was all that mattered.

Two hours later, the small private jet had landed, and they were sliding into a waiting SUV. As they rode the city streets, Lyriq's eyes sparkled with joy. She'd always wanted to visit Vegas but never had the opportunity. Now she was there with the man of her dreams, living in a way she'd only ever read about. It wasn't long before they were checking into an executive suite at The Palazzo.

"I still can't believe you arranged all of this just a few hours ago. It's all been magnificent," Lyriq gushed.

"It's not over yet, sweetheart. J-Lo has a special engagement tonight and we'll be there front and center."

Lyriq threw her arms around Ryker's neck, planted kisses all over his face. "I don't deserve you; I don't deserve any of this."

"That's where you're wrong, you deserve all of this and so much more. Now if you'll look in that closet, you'll find something I think will look extraordinary on you. If you like it, which I hope you will, please wear it tonight to dinner and the show."

Lyriq dashed off to the closet and pulled out a gorgeous, cream-colored Alexander McQueen dress and gold Jimmy Choo shoes. She couldn't help but laugh to herself and compare this moment to a scene from her favorite movie, *Pretty Woman*. She'd never been anyone's hooker, but Ryker was accepting her, past and all.

He Won't Go

The thought of sharing a shower with Lyriq excited Ryker more than he cared to admit, but he restrained himself and gave her privacy as she cleansed her body. Once she was safely tucked into a bath robe, he took to the bathroom to get ready for their evening. It wasn't long before they were dressed to the nines, ready to enjoy their special night. The black SUV dashed the foursome off to a five-star restaurant where they enjoyed a scrumptious meal. They raised their glasses in a toast as Kane offered up beautiful words about love and happiness. But Lyriq didn't hear a word he'd said, she was too tuned into Ryker and how handsome he looked in his suit, how good he smelled, how much she wanted to feel him inside her. When they all said cheers, she tossed back her wine, trying to douse the flame burning deep inside.

J-Lo did not disappoint. Her performance was full of energy, incredible dancing, and she sang all of their favorites. Lyriq didn't think the evening could get any better, but then Ryker announced that the night was still young, and they had one more stop to make. The driver pulled up in front of another hotel along the strip and held the door as they exited the vehicle. Hand-in-hand, they walked through the hotel until they arrived in front of an angelic set of doors. Kane stepped forward and opened the doors, revealing a chapel filled with beautiful flowers, soft music, and a minister standing underneath an archway. Lyriq turned to Mona, ready to congratulate her when Mona took her by the shoulders and turned her back around where she saw Ryker on one knee holding a box with a four-karat diamond ring. Tears spilled from her eyes as she nodded her acceptance. At the stroke of midnight, Lyriq became Mrs. Adams.

They returned to their hotel suite, but Lyriq couldn't even remember feeling her feet touch the ground. She was all smiles, floating on clouds, rejoicing, and giving thanks for her new relationship status. She was the Mrs. to a man she thought would never see her as wife material.

Ryker swung the door open and swooped his bride off her feet. He carried her across the threshold and into their room, decorated with what looked like a million candles and roses. Soft music wafted through the air, tangled with the scent of Jasmine. Lyriq couldn't have dreamt a more perfect day. Ryker stood her on her feet and never mumbling a word, he began to disrobe her. He unzipped her dress and let it fall in a puddle at her feet. With a smooth flick of his fingers, her bra was unhooked and quickly joined her dress on the floor. Ryker leaned down and kissed her deeply. He moved his hands down her curvaceous body until he reached her satin panties. He stooped down and slowly pulled them down her legs, steadying her while he lifted one foot at a time, until they were completely removed. Ryker ran his hand along the length of her right leg, kissing and gently sucking her smooth, warm thigh. Again, he resisted temptation and stood to his full height. He took a couple of steps back so he could admire his bride in all her glory. He was pleased that she didn't shy away from his glare, but instead welcomed him to stare at what now belonged to him. A mischievous smile played at the corners of his mouth as he began to remove his suit. By the time he'd gotten down to his boxer briefs, it was Lyriq who was smiling devilishly, taking in the thickness of her husband, from his broad chest to his excited soldier that was standing at full attention. Without shame or shyness, Ryker removed his briefs. He wanted to spin Lyriq around, bend her over the couch and take her from behind, right there in the living room, but this was their first time, their wedding night, it had to be special. So instead, he took her by the hand and led her to the rose petal covered bed, where he laid her down as if she were a fragile, porcelain doll. He traced her lips with his tongue before kissing her passionately. She met his kiss with great enthusiasm, clearly excited for what was about to take place. Ryker created a trail of kissed that made a brief stop at her neck, then down to her breasts, where he licked, gently bit, and teased her nipples. Lyriq arched her back and softly moaned her approval. Ryker continued his journey until he found her pleasure pearl. The scent of her drove him crazy as he pleasured her to her first orgasm. Then he pulled her on top of him and fought to control himself as she moved her hips rhythmically. He felt her body shudder as she erupted all over him, giving him permission to release his seed in an explosion of satisfaction.

CHAPTER 9

"I wish we didn't have to leave. I love this place for more reasons than I ever imagined I would," Lyriq confessed as she traced little circles on Ryker's chest with her fingertip. "You know we'll have to call our parents and tell them what we've done."

Ryker chuckled. "You sound scared. We're grown, baby, capable of making life decisions that they have no choice but to live with."

"But your mama is not going to be happy. I know because despite how much she tried to hide her uneasiness around me, it was still quite evident. She's probably freaked out that I came to visit you in the first place."

"I'm freaked out too. Freaked out by this smooth skin and juicy booty," he teased as he squeezed her bottom while positioning himself over her. They made love once more before getting up and preparing for their return flight to Irvine.

~~~

"Mama, I can't talk to you if you don't calm down. Now take a few breaths and calm yourself so we can have a conversation, or I'll hang up and call you back once I think you've settled down. Which will it be?"

He Won't Go

Constance took a deep breath and blew it out slowly. She was thankful Ryker couldn't see the tears streaming down her face. Despite his age, he was her baby, and she only wanted the best for him. At this point, she couldn't imagine Lyriq was good for him, she wasn't sure Lyriq knew what was best for herself. Yes, she'd overcome her addiction, but temptation was always right around the corner. Any slip-ups Lyriq had would negatively impart Ryker and that just didn't sit well with Constance.

"Ryker, I'm just trying to understand how you could fly her out there and marry her two days later. Was the sex that good, son?"

"Mama, how could you be so crude? And for the record, we didn't engage in any sexual activity until after we were married."

"So, you married her so you could have sex with her, and it be okay in the eyes of The Lord!" Constance exclaimed. "God is a forgiving God. You could've just screwed her and asked for forgiveness."

"Mama, you are out of line! I married Lyriq because I love her, and I know enough about God to know He's forgiven her for her transgressions and helped her to overcome her addiction. What I don't understand is how you've forgotten about the power of forgiveness, compassion, and God's ability to pull us through anything. You've turned your back on everything you taught me about God."

"I haven't forgotten, Ryker, but I do want what's best for you, and I don't think she's it. We know what drugs can do to a person, how it can destroy a family. Why would you want to live through that again?"

"Lyriq is not Daddy, she will not suffer his fate. You've got to stop looking at her through the same lens, she is not him. She is stronger, she is an overcomer, and together we will be unstoppable. Now you can either get on board with our marriage and support my wife, or cut us both out of your life, the choice is yours."

Constance cleared her throat and wiped her tears, "When can I expect you and my daughter-in-law to come home for a visit?"

"I'm working on closing a big deal but should have everything with it wrapped up by the end of the week. If that's the case, we'll be home for a few days next week to pack her things and ship them back out here."

"Can I plan a reception for you two while you're here?"

"That would be nice, Mama. I know Lyriq would appreciate it."

"Okay, baby. Just let me know for sure when you'll arrive and how long you'll be here."

"I will, and Mama, I love you. I hope you don't feel disrespected, you know I'd never want that. I simply wanted you to understand I'm serious about my marriage and I'm in love with my wife."

He Won't Go

"I understand, son, and I love you too."

Constance disconnected the call, picked up a snow globe, and threw it across the room as she let out a primal scream. The glass shattered into a thousand pieces, and she began to pray her son's new life wouldn't mimic that of the broken glass.

~~~

Kane raised his glass, signifying a toast. "Here's to you, Ryker. Your creativity, design, and attention to detail just landed us the deal of a lifetime. Once this building goes up, our firm will be the most sought after in the country. We'll have more business than we can handle. Congratulations on a job well done."

All the employees raised their glasses and shouted cheers. Ryker raised his own glass, said thanks, and tossed back the champagne. He shook hands and accepted the kind words from the staff before stepping away to his office. Once he was alone, he sat at his desk, bowed his head, and gave thanks for all the blessings that God was pouring into his life.

Wanting to celebrate his success with his wife, Ryker walked through the door carrying a huge bouquet of roses and a bottle of sparkling cider. But he nearly dropped everything when he crossed the threshold and saw Lyriq standing next to the candle lit table dressed in a red lace bra, thong, matching garter, and six-inch heels, holding a champagne flute.

"Cheers to the most talented architect in all of these United States," Lyriq gushed as she lifted her glass in his direction. "A talented man like yourself should be celebrated, so here, let's celebrate." She passed him a glass of cider and giggled as his eyes bulged out of his head.

Ryker placed the bottle of cider on the counter and exchanged the bouquet of roses for the champagne flute that Lyriq was offering. "You look absolutely amazing," he whispered as he leaned in for a kiss. "I didn't think my day could get any better and then I walked through that door to you, my wife, and I realized that with you, every day from here on out will be better than the day before." He sat the glass down, took Lyriq into his arms and didn't let go until morning.

CHAPTER 10

The SUV pulled up in front of Constance's home. Staring out the picture window, she inhaled deeply and said a little prayer. *Lord, please give me an understanding heart. I want to be supportive, but I'm so afraid of the pain she'll inflict upon my son. Help me, Lord, help me to see in Lyriq what Ryker sees.* She exhaled, put a smile on her face, and went outside to greet them.

Ryker lifted his mom off her feet and wrapped her in a warm embrace. "Hey Mama, how are you?"

"I'm better now that my baby is home." Constance kissed him on the cheek and then stepped to Lyriq. "Hello, my daughter," she sang as she gave Lyriq a tight squeeze. It was all she could do to keep from trying to crush the child until she disintegrated. Instead, she stepped back, looked at the happy couple and shook a motherly finger at them. "I can't believe what you two ran off and did. But what's done is done and now we prepare to celebrate. Come on in the house and let me fill you in on the celebratory plans."

Ryker took Lyriq by the hand as they followed Constance into the house. She had prepared a dinner of country fried streak, mashed potatoes and gravy, green beans, and rolls for them. As they stepped into the kitchen, she noticed that Ryker, aside from his bride's hand, was carrying nothing.

Stacey Covington-Lee

"Aren't you going to bring your bags in, Ryker? I've got the guest room all ready for you two. You'll be comfortable there, it's much better than your old room."

"Oh Mama, we don't want to put you out. We're staying at Lyriq's place in Macon."

"Nonsense, you'll stay here. I've prepared everything for you guys. Lyriq, your mom should be pulling up any minute and by the time we finish chatting and going over everything, it'll be too late to try and drive up to Macon." Making sure they knew her word was the final word, Constance blurted, "You're staying here!" Out of the corner of her eye she saw Lyriq look at Ryker and shrug her shoulders in defeat. Constance had won the first round.

Just as Constance had finished plating the food, Lyriq's mom, Paula, rang the doorbell. "Come on in," Constance shouted. "We're in the kitchen. You're just in time for dinner."

Paula raced over to her child and gave her a tight embrace. She then held Lyriq by the shoulders and stretched out her arms as if to examine a child just returning from war. "Look at my baby, a married woman," Paula gushed. "I, of course, wish I could've witnessed the blessed occasion, we both do," she said, nodding at Constance. "But we're thrilled you two have found love with one another."

"Speak for yourself," Constance mumbled.

"What was that, Constance?" Paula asked

62

He Won't Go

"I said I'm hungry. Let's eat before the food gets cold. We can discuss Saturday's celebration while we fill our bellies. Ryker, would you please bless the food?"

Ryker instructed everyone to hold hands and bow their heads. "Lord, we thank you for safe travels, for family and the love and understanding we all have for one another." He gave his mother's hand a squeeze before continuing. "We thank you for this delicious food and the loving hands that prepared it. In Jesus' name, amen."

The foursome ate and chatted about meaningless things. Finally, after everyone's stomach was full, Paula asked, "Since we couldn't be there, do you all at least have pictures of the wedding ceremony?"

Lyriq gushed as she whipped out her phone and showed the mothers photos that were snapped in the little Vegas wedding chapel. Both Constance and Paula were in awe of the beautiful dress Lyriq wore. As much as she wanted to hate on her new daughter-in-law, Constance had to admit the woman had made a beautiful bride and her son looked happier than she'd ever seen him. Even now, she looked across the table and saw him holding his bride's hand, smiling, and kissing her cheek. Constance said one more prayer, asking God to warm her heart to Lyriq and to be accepting of what she clearly couldn't change.

Constance and Paula filled the couple in on the reception plans they'd made. Lyriq thought two hundred guests were about one hundred too many, but she remained silent. The reception would take place in the most expensive Dublin event hall. They'd considered having it in the church gathering room, but the space was just too small. Dublin was only a twenty-minute ride south and the hall afforded them the space for a DJ, small dance floor, and buffet that included a separate carving station. Lyriq and Ryker may have denied their parents the opportunity to witness the marriage, but the mothers wouldn't be denied the chance to show off their kids and celebrate their union.

"Oh, Reverend Simon will be in attendance and has agreed to bless your union," Constance added. "Have you decided what you're going to wear?"

"I actually brought my wedding dress and thought I'd wear it for everyone to see. It's so beautiful, I don't want it to be a one and done dress. It deserves to be worn more than just once. Ryker will be in the same suit wore as well."

"Oh, it'll be like marrying all over again, only this time you'll be surrounded by loved ones," Paula exclaimed.

They finished discussing the details and Paula headed home. Constance stayed in the kitchen to clean up while Ryker and Lyriq went to gather their bags and prepare for bed. After everything was put away, counters wiped down and dishes washed, Constance headed to her room. As she passed the guest room, she heard the soft moans and groans of a couple trying unsuccessfully to make silent love. She shook her head, closed her door, and whispered, "God please don't let that child get pregnant."

He Won't Go

Constance was up early preparing breakfast when Lyriq came waltzing in the kitchen still scantily clad in a negligee that barely covered her butt.

"Guess I don't need to ask if you had a good night," Constance smirked.

"Nope, no need to ask, it was great. How was yours, did you sleep well, Ms. Constance?"

"I'd have slept better if you two weren't so noisy. As a proper young lady, you should be mindful of your behavior and noise level around others. It's the courteous thing to do."

Lyriq shot her mother-in-law a look full of disdain. She tried to hurry and check herself before responding. She didn't want to disrespect Constance, but the woman was pushing her buttons. "You're right, Ms. Constance, and that's why we'll be staying at my place in Macon for the remainder of this visit."

"Humph," Constance huffed.

"Would you kindly pass me a glass? Ryker would like some juice."

"Then Ryker should come into the kitchen and get it," Constance snapped.

"He's not dressed," Lyriq smirked. "The glass?"

Stacey Covington-Lee

Constance snatched a glass from the cabinet and placed it on the counter in front of Lyriq. "Here you go." Constance took a deep breath as Lyriq poured the juice. "May I ask you a question?"

"Of course."

"Everything with you and my son has moved so fast. Have you all discussed kids? Is that an aspect of your relationship that will move quickly as well?"

"We have not yet discussed children, Ms. Constance. That's a subject we'll broach when we feel the time is right. But let me put your mind at ease, I am on birth control." With that, Lyriq turned and walked back to her husband.

As the day rolled on, Ryker could feel the tension between his mom and his wife growing. He wasn't sure if Paula felt it or not, but if she did, like him, she did an excellent job of ignoring it. They did a walkthrough of the venue, approving all the decorations and met briefly with the good Reverend Jimmie Simon. As the ladies wrapped up the last few details, Ryker walked Jimmie out to his car.

"I guess you're just as surprised by our marriage as everyone else, huh?" Ryker asked.

Jimmie fished for his keys inside his pants pocket before offering a slight chuckle. "It wasn't hard to see how taken you were with her. While I was surprised to hear the news, none of us really should've been. I think the bigger question is, how will you get your wife and your mother on the same sheet of family love music?"

He Won't Go

"Man, if I knew the answer to that, I'd be the happiest man alive. My mom can't seem to get past Lyriq's past. She doesn't think Lyriq is good enough for me. She's worried that my wife will break my heart or worse yet, start using again," Ryker sighed deeply. "Any suggestions, Rev?"

"I suggest you pray," Jimmie offered before sliding in his car and taking off.

To Constance's dismay, Ryker and Lyriq took off for Macon once everything was finalized. They had a moving crew to meet them and help pack up the apartment. The same crew would be back the next evening after the reception to move the furniture to Lyriq's parents' basement. The boxes would be shipped, and the happy couple would spend their last night in a hotel.

~~~

The reception was absolutely beautiful. The happy couple's parents had pulled out all the stops. The decorations were gorgeous, the food was delectable, and the wedding cake was the most beautiful Lyriq had ever seen. With the guests seated, Ryker and Lyriq stood underneath a beautifully decorated arch with Reverend Jimmie. The good reverend blessed their rings, performed a brief religious ceremony, and prayed over their union. Now twice married to Ryker, Lyriq's heart was full, and no one could ever doubt the validity of their marriage or their commitment to one another. Not even her mother-in-law. Seeing firsthand how happy they were, Lyriq hoped this day would be the beginning of a better, more accepting relationship with Constance. The tension between them wore on Ryker and neither woman wanted him to suffer a second of stress.

Old high school friends, church members, and family friends congratulated the couple and enveloped them in love and support. A couple of Lyriq's old friends, Macie and Anna, had managed to corner her. They were curious about how she'd met Ryker, why they married so quickly, and if they should start planning a baby shower in the next few months.

"You know you've been prone to making mistakes in the past, but a baby with Ryker might be a mistake worth making," Macie teased.

Trying to hide her annoyance, Lyriq quipped, "We've all made mistakes. Macie, you know that better than most. But let me assure you, I'm not pregnant. Ryker loves me and that's why we're married. Now if and when we decide to have a baby, rest assured, you'll be the fifth or sixth to know."

Anna couldn't help but giggle at the shot Lyriq landed before turning and walking away, leaving Macie feeling like a petty fool.

"Laugh if you want to, Anna, but mark my words, her reign on top will come to an end soon enough. She'll screw this good thing up just as she has everything else in her drug induced life."

"Don't be ugly, Macie," Anna snipped. "Instead of waiting to relish in her downfall, why don't you pray for her marriage and

He Won't Go

happiness? God will reward your kindness, but remember, messiness has a reward too. A reward I want no part of." Anna walked away, leaving Macie to ponder her words.

After they'd greeted everyone, cut the cake, and danced their last dance, Lyriq and Ryker thanked everyone and took off for Macon. They needed to oversee things at her apartment and get checked into their hotel.

CHAPTER 11

"If we weren't so exhausted, I'd have suggested driving to Atlanta for the night. That would've made it easier to drop off the rental and make it to the airport with time to spare," Lyriq quipped as she fell back on the bed in their hotel room.

"Babe, we'll still have plenty of time for all of that. Besides, we promised our parents we'd try to make it down for brunch before heading back."

"That's a lot of back-tracking, Ryker."

"I know, but there's no telling how long it will be before we see them again. We're heading home, babe. I'll be swamped with work, you'll begin your job search, and before you know it, school will be in session and there will be no getting away for you until the holidays. Besides, after what they did for us yesterday, we can surely pay them one last visit."

Ryker pretended not to see her roll her eyes. He knew it was his mother she had no desire to see. But the fact of the matter was, they were family now and would have to learn to get along. As he grabbed his toiletry travel bag and headed for the bathroom, he decided that ignoring the tension was not a viable solution. Tomorrow he would address the women in his life and let them know his expectations for them all as a family.

He Won't Go

Lying in bed while Lyriq was in the shower, Ryker closed his eyes and prayed. *Father, please give me the words to relay to my wife and mother. We are a family now and I need You to create a sense of unity, peace, and love between us all.* As he prayed, he refused to entertain the thoughts that tried to creep into his head. He wouldn't listen to the little voice that suggested he may have moved too fast, that the marriage came too quickly. He loved Lyriq and he wanted her with him always. He knew it the moment he met her and wouldn't backtrack on any of that now.

In an effort to accommodate their children's travel schedule, Constance, Paula, and Bill skipped church and gathered at Constance's house for brunch. There was a wonderful spread of fresh fruits, scrambled eggs, hash browns, sausage, bacon, muffins, and Ryker's favorite, cheese grits. The smell of freshly brewed coffee greeted everyone at the door and Lyriq could hardly wait to pour a cup.

"Good morning, Ms. Constance," Lyriq smiled as she embraced her mother-in-law. "It smells like heaven in here."

"Well, come on in. I hope you two brought your appetites cause there's plenty of food," she sang with pride as she moved past Lyriq and hugged her son.

"I thought my parents would've been here by now," Lyriq questioned.

"Your mom called and said Bill had an upset stomach, but they'd be along as soon as they could," Constance explained.

"I swear, my dad has had stomach issues for as long as I can remember but refuses to see a doctor. He's as stubborn as a mule."

"While we wait for your parents, how about we head to the kitchen for some coffee?" Ryker suggested.

"Go ahead, I've got to make a stop at the lady's room," Lyriq said with a peck to Ryker's cheek.

Ryker and Constance moved on to the kitchen and started chatting over coffee. Ryker expressed his appreciation again for the beautiful reception. He'd also filled his mom in on all the work that he had waiting for him back in Irvine. "Once we're all settled in, Mom, I'd love for you to come out for a visit. It's been so long since you've spent time on the west coast."

"Humph, we'll have to see how your new bride feels about that," Constance shrugged. "Speaking of your bride, is she having tummy problems like her dad?"

"She has been gone a while."

"Keep drinking your coffee, son. I'll go check on her," Constance said as she pushed herself away from the table and headed down the hall. She turned the corner only to see Lyriq in her bedroom looking over family photos that weren't intended for public consumption. Constance stomped into her bedroom and snatched the photos from Lyriq's hands. "I know Paula and Bill taught you better

72

than to invade people's privacy. You shouldn't even be in my room, let alone rummaging through my things."

Lyriq looked like a deer caught in headlights. "I'm so sorry, Ms. Constance. I swear, I didn't mean to pry. I just saw the photo of your husband as I passed by, and curiosity took over. I wanted to see up close what he looked like. Ryker has no pictures of his father and has never discussed him at all."

"I understand your curiosity but stepping into my bedroom was stepping too far. If you married a man who hasn't been comfortable enough with you to share every aspect of his life, then maybe you married him too soon!" Constance spoke more harshly and loudly than she intended. "Open your mouth, speak to your husband, do whatever you need to do, but do not invade my privacy again."

"What's going on back here?" Ryker quizzed as he rounded the corner. "Mom, why are you yelling?"

"Ask your wife. I'll be in the kitchen and would appreciate it if you escorted her out of my bedroom." Constance huffed off as her blood boiled with anger.

"Babe, what happened? Why are you in my mom's bedroom?"

"I didn't mean to disrespect her or invade her space. I was passing by and saw this picture. You look just like him and I figured it was your father. I guess curiosity got the best of me. I just wanted to see a glimpse into your past. I wanted to learn something about your dad."

"This is not the way!" Ryker was sterner than Lyriq had ever heard before. "If you have questions about my life, my past, we can discuss them when we get back, but snooping through my mom's things is not an option. Now let's go eat while you apologize to my mother." Ryker grabbed her by the hand and led her to the kitchen.

As they passed the front door, the bell rang. Ryker stopped and welcomed Paula and Bill into his mom's house. They all made their way to the kitchen, where Constance was still stewing. Paula and Bill greeted Constance warmly, but the chill they received in return was off putting. The pair looked at one another as if to question what happened before their arrival.

Paula adjusted in her seat, uncomfortable in the thick fog of tension that enveloped the room. "Ok, can someone please fill us in on what's going on? Clearly, there's some issue that's driving a wedge between you and Constance," Paula said, with a nod in Lyriq's direction. "And poor Ryker looks like a lamb caught in barbed wire. He knows he has to move but is sadly tangled in a mess."

"If that's not an accurate description, I don't know what is," Ryker mumbled.

Lyriq cleared her voice and tried to explain what had transpired a few moments ago. As she talked, a look of disbelief set itself upon her mother's face. Lyriq finally stopped trying to explain and turned to Constance to offer a sincere, heartfelt apology. Constance gave a halfhearted acceptance and began preparing plates for everyone.

He Won't Go

"I'm sorry if the eggs aren't exactly hot, but the coffee is hot, and the juice is chilled. Please eat up and enjoy," Constance said as she tried to sound more cheerful. The atmosphere finally began to take on a lighter feel. The fog was replaced with conversation and laughter. Once everyone's bellies were full and the clock signified a need to hit the road, Ryker and Lyriq kissed their parents and bid them goodbye.

The ride to the airport and flight home to Irvine was much quieter than normal. They both contemplated the conversation they knew would have to happen once they were settled back in their place.

~~~

Three days had passed since their return and the honeymooners still hadn't broached the conversation about the incident at Constance's house, the details of Ryker's deceased father, or his youth that she knew so little about. At a loss as to what to do next, Lyriq decided to head to the café on the corner for some good coffee and maybe a new perspective. She whipped out her phone and called Bailey to see if she was available for brunch. Thankfully, she was and told Lyriq she'd meet her at the café in thirty minutes.

Lyriq walked in the door and was immediately spotted by the motherly waitress from her last visit.

"Good morning, sweetheart, grab that table in the corner and I'll be right with you," the waitress said with a nod at the table.

Lyriq settled into the seat and began to peruse one of the menus left on the table. Her mind drifted to how she and Ryker hadn't made love since returning. Their conversations hadn't consisted of more than *hi*, *bye*, and *are you hungry*. She'd apologized for the incident at his mother's house...again. She'd told him if he'd just discuss his childhood with her, she wouldn't have to wonder or imagine the worst. She was starting to feel a little resentful of his coldness. She'd been an open book with him, she'd allowed herself to be vulnerable, yet he wasn't willing to do the same. Where was the fairness in that? Her husband and his lack of communication consumed her thoughts began to cause her to doubt their decision to marry.

"Man trouble?" The waitress asked as she sat an extra sweet caramel latte down in front of Lyriq.

"How did you know and how did you remember my drink?"

"I've been here a long time, sweetheart. I know that look and I never forget a drink," the waitress replied.

"Thanks for the latte and by the way, my name is Lyriq."

"Oh, that's pretty. Now, what would you like to eat, sweetheart?"

Lyriq shook her head with a halfhearted giggle. "I'm expecting someone, so I'll wait for her and place our orders together."

"Oh good. Nothing like a friend to share a meal with. Just be careful you're not sharing too much too soon with your friends. People can disguise themselves as one thing and be something totally

76

different. Be sure to figure out if you're talking to the one thing or the different thing. I'll be back to check on you." With that, she sashayed away, leaving Lyriq scratching her head at the weird advice.

Lyriq was thumbing through her phone when she heard a cheerful voice approach.

"Hey girl, welcome back. It's good to see you," Bailey sang as she bent down and planted a friendly kiss on Lyriq's cheek. She slid into the booth opposite her brunch companion and started firing off questions. "So how was the whole reception thing? Did you guys get everything moved out here or will you have to make a return trip? Most importantly, are the families as happy about your union as you two are?"

"Girl, I'm going to need you to slow it down a tad. You're super hyped this morning and I can't say that your hype mixes well with my chill right now."

"Whatever, just answer my questions."

Before Lyriq could respond, the waitress returned to take their orders. Lyriq got the French toast again, while Bailey settled for a chocolate-covered donut and vanilla latte. Once the waitress turned and walked away, Lyriq sighed deeply and gave Bailey a rundown of the weekend. She described the beauty of the wedding celebration, how they'd successfully gotten everything moved and lastly, how she'd gotten busted snooping in Constance's room.

Stacey Covington-Lee

"I hate that I overstepped, but I just really wanted to find anything concerning Ryker and his father. I've been an open book with him, but he still hasn't opened up to me. Since returning, we haven't had any real conversation at all. Our marriage is so new, and I don't want this to ruin it."

The motherly waitress sat Bailey's vanilla latte on the table in front of her and just happened to catch the tail end of what Lyriq was saying while doing so. As she turned to walk away, she heard Bailey offer up her best advice.

"Sex him, girl. When he comes home, jump his bones, put it on him good and watch things improve."

The waitress paused briefly, shook her head, and continued on to check on her other tables.

"What was that about?" Bailey asked with a slight attitude.

"I have no idea, probably had nothing to do with our conversation at all." Lyriq smirked although she knew better. "Do you really think a romantic evening is enough to get us back on track?"

"Well, it certainly can't hurt. At the very least, it'll relax you both and make talking about the important stuff a little easier," Bailey assured.

Their food arrived and Lyriq giggled at the side of eggs that accompanied her French toast and lack of anything to balance out Bailey's donut. While they ate, the pair continued to talk about

78

everything and nothing at all. They giggled like schoolgirls over Bailey's stories of the passengers that offered her the moon for one night of intimacy. Lyriq's giggles turned to astonishment when Bailey whispered about the offers she'd accepted from two old men.

"Girl, I needed the money, and those tips were not cutting it," she laughed. "Anyway, I have to pick up a passenger in twenty minutes, so I'd better get a move on."

Bailey reached in her purse for money, but Lyriq insisted on paying for her small meal. Bailey slid out of her seat, offered her appreciation for the free snack, and turned to leave. She didn't get far before turning on her heels and dashing back to the table.

"I forgot to ask; I'm driving to Los Angeles this weekend for a little shopping. If you and hubby don't have plans, why don't you ride with me? We can have a great lunch, hit the Beverly Center and Rodeo Drive," she sang out, trying to entice Lyriq.

"That actually sounds great. I'll give you a call and let you know."

"All right, talk to you later." Bailey turned to leave and slowed her pace as she passed the waitress. The waitress raised an eyebrow at her but kept on stepping.

"Can I get you anything else, sweetheart?" The waitress asked.

"No thank you, I'm stuffed."

Stacey Covington-Lee

"Well, here's the check, I'll take it whenever you're ready. And not that it's any of my business, but that advice your friend gave you has got to be the worst I've ever heard."

"And what would you advise, Ms.... Oh wow, I don't even know your name," Lyriq realized.

"The name's Betty and I would advise that you sit down and talk openly and honestly with your husband. You all are young, with all the time in the world to be intimate, but that intimacy won't mean a thing if you can't sit down and talk through your troubles. But what do I know? I'm just an old waitress." She grinned as she picked up the credit card Lyriq had placed on top of the check.

When Ms. Betty returned with the card and receipt, Lyriq thanked her, added a big tip to the check before signing it, and headed home. She walked slowly and mulled over the advice both Bailey and Ms. Betty had offered. Regardless of whose advice she chose to take, she knew she needed to set the mood. Detouring from her walk home, Lyriq stopped by the grocery store and picked up a couple of steaks, baking potatoes, and a cheesecake. Regardless of what happened tonight, it would happen with full stomachs. Her husband was a big man that enjoyed a satisfying meal. The least she could do was provide him that.

CHAPTER 12

Ryker was mentally exhausted from his busy workday. All he wanted was to go home to a warm, peaceful environment, not the strained one he and Lyriq had been sharing since returning home. He parked his car in the garage, sat for a moment and whispered a prayer. *"Father, please give me the strength, the patience, and the words to fix things with my wife."* He exhaled deeply and headed up to their condo.

To his great surprise, Ryker entered the condo to find his wife standing beside a beautifully decorated table, with a warm smile stretched across her face. She was dressed in a casual maxi dress with gold-toned sandals and her hair loosely pulled back into a ponytail. She was beautiful and as appealing as she was to the eye, whatever she was cooking was just as appealing to his sense of smell. He moved further into their home and without speaking a word, he took Lyriq into arms and held her like he never wanted to let go.

"Welcome home, husband. I hope you brought your appetite with you," Lyriq said as she planted a kiss on his cheek.

"I sure did! Haven't eaten a thing all day and the aroma in here has kicked my taste buds into high gear."

"Poor baby," Lyriq moaned with a poked-out lip. "Well, get comfortable and wash up while I plate the food. We can eat and you can tell me all about your day."

Ryker did as he was told and then the pair sat down to a delicious dinner. Lyriq smiled as she watched her husband gobble up everything she'd prepared. It made her feel good to see him enjoy her food as much as he enjoyed anything his mom had prepared. Once they were done with the main course, she swapped out their sweet tea for ice water and served up thick slices of cheesecake with strawberry topping. When neither could hold another bite, she cleared the table and joined Ryker outside on the terrace. She laid on the lounge chair beside his and reached for his hand.

"Babe, I really am sorry for rifling through your mother's things and I swear, I'll find a way to make it up to her, to get back in her good graces. I saw the photo of your dad and it just made me more desperate to know about him, you two's relationship, your family life before his passing." Lyriq squeezed his hand a little tighter. "I've bared my soul to you, answered every question you've asked, but when it comes to your life prior to your dad's death, I'm completely in the dark. I know it's probably painful for you to talk about him, but it's also important for me to know everything that made you the man you are today. I want to know everything about my husband, the good, bad, and the ugly."

With a deep sigh, Ryker resigned himself to share the love and the shame of his dad, Cyrus Adams. He told his wife about the giggles shared between his parents when his dad would swirl his mom around the kitchen as if they were on a dance floor in a club. He told her how he and his dad bonded over fishing trips and baseball. He smiled as he recalled their one big vacation to Disney World, with some of his aunts, uncles, and cousins. He let her know that before death, there was joy, but there were also arguments. His mom screaming at the top of her lungs and throwing things at his dad, but it wasn't until his dad's death that he found out why his mom held such anger towards his father.

"Shortly after we were notified of dad's murder, the rumor mill blew word to my mom that it was his mistress' husband that beat and killed him," Ryker confessed. "My mom had known of his affair and threatened to leave a million times. She also knew the thing that connected him to his mistress was more the drugs than the sex. She never felt there was a love connection between them, but the woman would plow him with drugs and my dad's addiction wouldn't let him leave her."

"Wow, I had no idea that your father was hooked on drugs. That explains so much about why your mom is less than thrilled about your marrying me. I can imagine she'd be afraid of me dragging you to the dark side like that woman did your father," Lyriq assumed.

"I'd like to say you're wrong, but you hit the nail on the head."

Lyriq dropped her husband's hand and brought her palms to her face. She held her head as it shook from side to side. "Here I am, a recovering addict, married to Constance's one and only child. She must be horrified by the possibility of my corrupting you."

Reaching out and taking her hand back in his, Ryker kissed it and assured her, "There's no need for you to worry about my mom. Your job is to be my wife, to help me make a good life for us. My mom is my concern."

Lyriq smiled at his reassurance. "Babe, I hate to keep making you re-live everything, but the guy that killed your dad, did he catch him in bed with his wife and shoot him, or what exactly happened?"

"Apparently, my dad used to park his truck in the driveway of an abandoned house several yards from his mistress' home. Late one night, her husband saw him walking to his truck, turned the wheel of his vehicle and aimed straight for my dad. He barely bumped him with the car, but my dad was so high he couldn't get to his feet. The guy grabbed a baseball bat and beat my father to death. He left him right there in the road like a dead dog."

"Unbelievable. Babe, I'm so sorry. No human should ever die like that. I can't imagine the pain this caused you and your mom. I just hope the pain was eased by the knowledge that the murderer will rot in prison," Lyriq offered in comfort.

"That man is still married to his wife, living in the same house, driving on the same road where he killed my father."

Lyriq sat straight up, shocked by Ryker's revelation. "How can that be?"

He Won't Go

Ryker turned his head as he wiped an escape tear from his cheek. He cleared his throat and turned back to face his wife. "The woman my father was cheating with was white. Her husband was white. This happened in rural, middle Georgia that, as you know, still has its prejudices. I mean, the town is still separated by race for goodness' sake. And with no eyewitnesses, the white sheriff, who happened to be the murderer's cousin, swept the whole thing under the rug. Never mind that the guy was heard around town bragging about killing my dad, they swore they didn't have enough evidence for an arrest."

Choking back tears, Lyriq moved over to Ryker's chair and wrapped her arms around him. She soaked his chest with her tears as he tried unsuccessfully to keep his own from rolling. He took comfort in his wife's arms, and she appreciated his willingness to be vulnerable and share the pain he'd clearly tucked away years ago. Lyriq understood her mother-in-law's concerns but was moved beyond words at how open Ryker's heart was to her, despite both their pasts. She knew that if she did nothing else in life, she had to honor her husband by staying clean and sober and being a stronger person than his father was able to be.

CHAPTER 13

Lyriq's interview with the school board went better than she ever imagined. She was offered a position at the middle school within walking distance of the condo. They even granted her an extra ninety days to complete their state licensing requirements. She had to stop herself from dancing out of the building. Once outside, she let out a little squeal as she jumped into the car and drove straight to Ryker's office. She walked through the building, greeting everyone she encountered. Everyone was warm and welcoming, including Kane, who greeted her with a peck on the cheek after she mistakenly interrupted a meeting between him and Ryker when she burst into Ryker's office unannounced.

"It's wonderful to see you, Kane, but please forgive my rudeness. Ryker, I'm going to hang out in the reception area. Please get me when you're done."

"Nonsense," Kane belted. "We were just finishing up. Please stay and let me leave, otherwise your husband will keep me in here far past lunch and I'm hungry," he said with a chuckle. "Ryker, we'll talk again before we leave for the day. Have a good afternoon, you two." Kane exited the office, closing the door behind him.

"I wasn't expecting you until later. I thought you'd be out exploring all day after dropping me off this morning," Ryker stated as he moved around his large desk to give his wife a hug and a kiss. "What brings you back so soon?"

"I didn't tell you, but the reason I wanted the car today was so I could go for an interview and babe, they hired me right away. I'll be teaching at Middleton Middle School when the fall session begins," Lyriq proclaimed as she bounced up and down like a gleeful child.

Sweeping her up into a bear hug, Ryker spun her around and told her just how proud he was of her. She gave him all the details of the interview and naturally wanted to celebrate her accomplishment.

"What do you say we take a day trip tomorrow? Do some sightseeing, maybe a little shopping, have a picnic on the beach. What do you say? Sounds great, right?"

"It sounds wonderful, but," Ryker's voice trailed off as he squinted his face, preparing to deliver the disappointing news.

"But what?" Lyriq smirked.

"But Kane and I are playing golf tomorrow with a potentially big client. There's a new course the guy says he's been dying to play so we offered, and he accepted. With guys like this, the golf course is where big deals are sealed. I'm sorry, sweetie, but I promise to make it up to you. I'll take you out for a phenomenal dinner tomorrow night, with maybe a surprise sprinkled in. How does that sound?"

"Sounds like it'd better be a lovely surprise," Lyriq half-joked. "Oh well, I guess I'll take Bailey up on her offer to hang out in L.A. and meet you back at home in time for dinner."

Ryker pulled back from Lyriq's embrace. "Who is Bailey?"

"The driver I told you about, remember? The one you had booked for me when I first got here."

"Oh yeah. Cool, you can shop for some new school clothes," he teased.

The pair exchanged a few more words and a kiss before Lyriq left, allowing him to give his work his full attention.

~~~

Ryker stepped from the shower and wrapped a towel around his waist. He looked in the mirror and decided a shave wasn't necessary for the day. He was about to start his grooming ritual when Lyriq stepped into the bath. Without saying a word, she reached for his towel and pulled it from his waist. She let it fall to the floor as she admired his thick physique. A smile teased at the corners of her lips and the gleam in her eye was all the invitation Ryker needed. He stepped to her and with the tips of his fingers, he slid the straps of her slinky gown from her shoulders and watched as it dropped to the floor. He tilted his head and took in every inch of Lyriq's soft yet toned body. He ran his fingers through her hair and cupped the back of her head, brought his lips to hers and kissed her passionately. It was as if she could feel the transfer of love between them. But the love quickly became lustful. Their breath blended together into an intoxicating cocktail as Ryker palmed her hips and sat her on the bathroom vanity. Ryker placed her legs on his shoulders as he kneeled to feast on her sweetness. With every lick, every tease of his tongue, Lyriq's body shuddered with excitement. Standing to his full height, he allowed her legs to land in the bends of his arms. He kissed her again, allowing her to taste her sweetness as he gently entered her sugar walls. The in and out motion escalated from sweet and gentle to deep, pounding, rhythmic thrusts. When he felt Lyriq tighten her walls around him and shudder in satisfaction, he allowed himself to explode in complete ecstasy.

"How do you expect me to play a decent game of golf after that?" Ryker huffed as he tried to catch his breath.

"Your golf game was the last thing on my mind," she snickered.

Ryker began placing soft kisses all over her face and neck as he eased out of her. He slid her off the vanity and walked her to the shower. They confirmed their plans as they bathed one another. They stepped from the shower and prepared for the day.

"So what time is Bailey picking you up?"

"She should be here within the hour. I've already told her I need to be back by six. That gives us both all day to play and not be rushed for our eight o'clock reservation."

"Sounds good, sweetie. I love you and I'll meet you back here by six," Ryker confirmed as he leaned in and gave her a goodbye kiss.

~~~

"Girl, you've got your head out that window looking like a dog that's been deprived a joy ride for far too long," Bailey laughed almost uncontrollably. She was often cracked up by her own corny jokes.

"Stop laughing at me. I've never seen any of this before, I'm just trying to take it all in. You should be glad I'm enjoying the ride."

"I am. I love seeing your excitement and by the way, I'm laughing with you, not at you. There's a big difference."

"Yeah, whatever. Ooh, I love that song. Turn it up!" Lyriq bellowed as she began to dance in her seat.

Bailey sped down the highway as she listened to Lyriq sing her heart out. There was no denying it, the girl had an incredible voice. Bailey found herself dangling between feelings of envy and those of admiration. Lyriq was not only beautiful, but she was basking in the joy of a happy marriage, had just landed a good job, and if that weren't enough, the girl had the voice of an angel. Bailey pressed past her temporary feelings of jealousy and decided to enjoy the beauty of her friend.

"I can't believe you'd settle for being a teacher when you have a voice like that. Have you not ever considered a singing career?" Bailey quizzed.

"I thought about it once upon a time but decided that I was called to share my gift in church. Occasionally, I would get to sing at school events with the kids, but I really like being a teacher. Besides, the congregation back home always made me feel like a superstar and that's enough for me."

"A voice like that was meant to be shared with the world, not just some country church."

"What we're not going to do is talk badly about my church," Lyriq blurted out defensively. She realized her so-called "country church" helped to save her, embraced her after her fall from grace, and continued to support her.

Bailey raised her hands as if to concede before placing them back on the wheel. "Sorry, my bad. I certainly didn't mean to offend. I was simply saying your voice is beautiful. The entire world should hear you sing."

"Thank you, Bailey, and I'm sorry for popping off on you. I'm just very protective of home, I guess."

"No worries, I understand."

The ladies continued their ride with the sounds of Pop and R&B music as their backdrop. A few songs later and they exited the 405 freeway and began maneuvering the L.A. streets. Again, Lyriq was looking around like an excited child taking a tour of the world's largest toy store. Bailey glanced over and smiled at the excitement plastered across Lyriq's face. It wasn't long before she was parallel parking on the famous Rodeo Drive.

Stacey Covington-Lee

"Girl, we've got about two miles of high-end shops, where do you want to start?" Bailey quizzed.

"Let's look in Bally shoe store first, shoes are my weakness."

The ladies started in Bally, but sticker shock sent Lyriq running right back out. That was the case with every store she entered. Bailey already knew how outrageously priced everything was, but she assumed because of Lyriq's new marital status and the success of her husband, she'd be spending money like water. Clearly, she was mistaken. While Lyriq is a classically styled woman, her high-end look is achieved on a budget.

"I refuse to leave this street without having purchased something from the famous Rodeo Drive," Lyriq asserted as she dragged Bailey into the Chanel store. "This is super cute, and I know I'll get plenty of wear out of it."

"It's a freaking t-shirt, Lyriq. I thought you were going to splurge."

"Excuse you, it's a two-hundred-and-fifty-dollar t-shirt! And please believe I'm going to wear the letters off of this thing," Lyriq asserted.

As the women got back in the car, Bailey turned to Lyriq thoughtfully. "Would you mind if we hit The Beverly Center on out next trip? I have somewhere I'd really like to take you. I promise we won't be long, and I'll have you back in plenty of time for your celebratory dinner."

92

He Won't Go

"Sure, let's go."

Bailey blasted the music, whipped the car around, and took off in the opposite direction. Lyriq sang at the top of her lungs as she watched the landscape change before her eyes. They left Beverly Hills behind and maneuvered the streets of the more modest Culver City. A few more turns and Bailey parked at what looked like a small industrial strip mall.

"You ready?" She asked gleefully.

"Ready for what?" Lyriq asked with confusion etched in her face.

"You'll see. Come on, let's go."

Lyriq felt a little uneasy as she followed her friend into a small store front marked Sound Notes. The tiny front lobby was decorated in cheesy oversized beanbags and a tacky coffee table with scattered pieces of candy you'd find in your grandma's candy dish. Then Bailey tapped on a large, heavy black door and eased it open without waiting for anyone to yell come in. As they stepped over the threshold, a fully equipped, professional music studio came into view and Lyriq's anxiety skyrocketed.

"Why are we in a studio?" She asked as she tugged at Bailey's shirt sleeve.

"Chill, Lyriq, I just wanted to introduce you to an old friend who happens to be in the music industry," she replied as shook Lyriq off her arm as if she were a worrisome puppy. She moved further into the room and threw herself into the arms of a tall, lanky, fair-skinned man with wavy hair. "Rogan, this is my girl, Lyriq. Lyriq, this is a dear old friend that's as talented as he is handsome."

Lyriq extended her hand. "Hello, Rogan, it's nice to meet you."

"Same here," he replied with a certain gleam in his eye that made Lyriq even more uncomfortable. "What brings you lovely ladies by?"

"Lyriq has an incredible voice and I thought it would be fun if you recorded her singing a couple of verses and let her have a copy...please."

"Are you seriously interrupting valuable studio time so you two can goof around?"

"He's right," Lyriq nodded to Bailey. "Now, let's get out of here," she said as she turned and started to walk away.

Bailey grabbed Lyriq by the arm and pulled her back. "Don't be like that, Rogan, this will literally take ten minutes of your time, if that."

Blowing out an exasperated breath, Rogan flatly agreed. "Fine... Lyriq, step in the booth and sing whatever you like. Please sing directly into the mic and enunciate. No muddled words, please."

Lyriq took several deep breaths as she moved towards the booth. She whispered to herself, "This is just for fun. It's not like last time, it's just for fun." She closed the door to the booth, took another cleansing breath and began to belt out the classic Yolanda Adams song, "Be Blessed."

Rogan, who had been slouching in his chair, sat straight up. He couldn't believe his ears. Bailey, on the other hand, just smiled as his reaction confirmed what she already knew…Lyriq had mad talent. They listened intently, although her song choice wasn't one either of them was familiar with. Lyriq ended her song and before she could fully step out of the booth, Rogan was laying her vocals over background music. The tune was different from that of the original song, but it sounded just as amazing, if not a little better. Lyriq was giddy as she listened to the playback.

"Young lady, I owe you an apology. I thought my girl Bailey was wasting my time, but this was quite the opposite. Your voice is incredible, and I'd love to work with you. I have writers on standby that could come up with the perfect song to accentuate your voice. What do you say?"

Lyriq smiled from ear to ear. "Thank you so much for the offer, but I'm a schoolteacher that reserves singing for Sunday morning church service."

Rogan popped a flash drive out of his computer and handed it to Lyriq. He then reached in a drawer to retrieve a couple of other items. Lyriq was busy fondling the flash drive and thinking about how she couldn't wait to play it for Ryker. Then it hit her, the scent of marijuana. She snatched her head up to see Rogan exhaling a huge bloom of smoke as he passed the blunt to Bailey. Lyriq began to shake as her past all came rushing back to her. She dropped the flash drive as she turned and ran out of the building. Bailey found her outside, leaning against the car with tears rolling down her face.

"What's the matter with you? One minute you're as happy as can be and the next you're running out like some freaking lunatic." Bailey's annoyance was completely unmasked.

"I need to go home now!"

"What the hell is wrong with you?"

"Now, Bailey, take me home now!" Lyriq barked as she got in the car.

Understanding nothing but her own anger, Bailey got in the car and sped all the way back to Irvine. Not a word was spoken the entire way. Both women sat steaming in their own thoughts, anger, and embarrassment. Bailey came to a screeching halt in front of Lyriq's building. Lyriq grabbed her purse and shopping bag. As she pulled at the door handle, Bailey dropped the flash drive of the recording into her bag. Neither said goodbye, Lyriq simply disappeared into her building.

CHAPTER 14

Lyriq struggled to get her mind out of that recording studio and focused on preparing for her evening with Ryker. She rummaged through her closet for something casual with a touch of elegance. She settled on a sleeveless, black jumpsuit and black stilettos. With the jumpsuit hanging outside her closet and shoes resting underneath, Lyriq disrobed and pulled her hair up into a loose bun. She turned on the shower and while she waited for the water to get hot, she looked at her reflection in the full-length mirror. She admired her toned, curvaceous body. She loved the way she looked now versus years ago when drugs ravaged her body and had her looking like a zombie from *The Walking Dead*. Her skin had a beautiful, healthy glow, her hair healthy and bouncy, her eyes clear.

"This is the woman Ryker loves, not who you were then. He could never love her. Remember that, always remember that," she said to her reflection.

She stepped into the shower and began to lather her body. When her mind drifted again to the studio and the aroma of the marijuana, she pulled the loofah to her nose and inhaled deeply, trying to let the scent of her jasmine body wash overtake the memory of the weed. She was so focused on trying to clear her head, she hadn't heard Ryker enter the bathroom. When he opened the shower door, she almost jumped out of her skin.

Ryker moved behind Lyriq and wrapped his arms around her. "I didn't mean to scare you, my angel. I thought you'd heard me coming in. When I saw you in here bathing, I couldn't resist joining you. I hope you don't mind."

Turning to face her husband, a warm smile stretched across her face and the sparkle returned to her eyes. "Of course, I don't mind," she said as she kissed his lips. Her gentle kisses quickly became deeper and more passionate. She forced herself to pull away and slow things down. "Pass me your towel so I can bathe you," she instructed as she nibbled at his ear.

The pair was able to contain their desires long enough to finish showering and dressing for the evening. Once in her jumpsuit, Lyriq completed her ensemble with a pair of diamond stud earrings and a gold necklace with a sizable Swarovski crystal that hung midway her cleavage. She'd achieved her casual, yet elegant look. Ryker was just as stylish in his dark jeans, blue button-down shirt, dark tan blazer, and matching tan loafers. Shortly after heading out, Ryker pulled into a parking space outside one of Irvine's finest five-star restaurants. As soon as they entered the doors, the hostess welcomed them and ushered them to towards the back.

"Babe, why is she bringing us back here? You hate sitting in the back," Lyriq whispered.

"Most times I do, but not tonight, love."

He Won't Go

The hostess opened the kitchen doors and off to the left was a beautifully set table, with a centerpiece of fragrant, exotic flowers. A waiter was standing by the table, poised and ready to cater to their every culinary whim. The maître d' quickly stepped forward and pulled out a chair.

"Ma'am," he said as he offered the seat to Lyriq. He stepped to the center of the table once the couple was seated and went over the four-course meal being prepared specifically for them. It consisted of all of Lyriq's favorites. He then presented them with a bottle of sparkling cider and poured a glass for each, before stepping away from the table.

"I can't believe you did all of this. I thought this kind of treatment was reserved for the rich and famous." Lyriq blushed.

"Well, you're famous to me, babe, and nothing is too good for you," Ryker boasted as he raised his glass in a toast to his bride and her new career move.

The waiter placed bowls of French onion soup before them and Lyriq's eyes lit up. "You really do know me," she blushed.

"Isn't that my job?" Ryker countered with a sly grin. "Later, I'm going to show you some other things I've learned about you, you know, like teasing that spot that makes you moan."

"I'm going to need you to behave before someone hears you."

"Woman, we're grown and married. I don't care who hears us," he chuckled loudly.

The meal continued with a delicious appetizer of crab cakes and an entrée of filet medallions with crispy lobster. The dessert portion was more than either could hold at the time, so they opted to take the chocolate-glazed Boston cream whoopie pies home. Ryker surmised they'd need the strength of those pies after they enjoyed one another at home. Lyriq blushed at his summation like a shy schoolgirl all while her body tingled with anticipation. The head chef came over to ensure they'd enjoyed every bite of their special meal. The happy couple gushed over the food, Ryker paid the tab, handsomely tipped all the servers, and practically ran out the door trying to get home.

Feeling a love hangover from the previous night, Ryker dragged himself out of bed, giving Lyriq a gentle shake as he stood and stretched. "Come on, love, church starts in a little while and you know you don't like to be rushed."

"Babe, I'm so tired from last night. Can't we skip today?"

"Love, we've yet to go to church since we got back. Trust me, I want to lay lazily in your love, but we've got to go give thanks and praise to The Almighty. He's been too good to us. Besides, I want you to meet your new church family."

Lyriq moaned and kicked the covers as if she were a child about to throw a tantrum. She looked up at Ryker and rolled her eyes in annoyance.

He Won't Go

Ryker bent down and pecked her on the cheek. "Service is only an hour and a half. We'll stop for brunch afterwards then come home and binge your favorite *Netflix* shows."

The look of annoyance never left Lyriq's face, but she did finally concede by dragging herself into the shower. Within the hour, they were pulling out of the garage and heading to Victory Land Christian Center. Despite Lyriq's initial annoyance, the spirit-filled service soon washed over her and made her grateful for the opportunity to sing praises unto The Lord. When service ended, Ryker took a few minutes to introduce Lyriq to some of the other parishioners, as well as the minister. Everyone was very welcoming, especially Pastor Carlton, who'd encouraged her to get involved with the church as her comfort level permitted. As they turned to leave, Lyriq jumped back a little at the sight of Rogan standing before her.

"Hey, if it isn't the songbird," Rogan smiled broadly. "It's good to see you again." He then extended his hand to Ryker. "Hey man, how are you? I'm Rogan."

"Nice to meet you, Rogan, I'm Lyriq's husband, Ryker Adams. If you don't mind my asking, where do you two know each other from?"

"Lyriq didn't tell you about the song she recorded in my studio yesterday? Man, your wife has an amazing voice."

With all eyes on her, Lyriq stood dumbfounded. The men exchanged a couple more pleasantries and Rogan apologized to

Ryker for freaking his wife out. Still shaken by Rogan's presence, Lyriq told Ryker she wasn't feeling well and wanted to leave. Confused by the entire interaction, Ryker took his wife by the hand and led her out to the car.

As he merged into traffic, Ryker glanced over at Lyriq, who was still looking ill. "Babe, you want to fill me in on what all that was about? How did you meet him and land in his studio? More importantly, why didn't you tell me about any of it?"

Lyriq adjusted herself in the seat, unable to get comfortable. It wasn't that she was trying to hide anything from her husband, but the thought of Rogan and the studio brought thoughts of the weed, its smell, and how elevated it probably would've made her feel. She shook her head, trying to free herself of the thoughts. "I didn't mean to keep anything from you, love, but we got so caught up in our celebration last night and church this morning, I simply hadn't had a chance to speak on it." She recounted her day of shopping with Bailey, and her friend's sweet gesture of having her record a song at Rogan's studio. She told him how all was going well until Rogan pulled out a blunt and she freaked out and ran. Ryker just drove in silence. Once they were back in the condo, Lyriq inserted the flash drive she'd found in her bag into the computer. She played the recording for Ryker, who listened and smiled.

"He's right, you know, you do have an amazing voice."

"Thank you, love, but the blunt incident reminded me of the pitfalls of music and why it's an aspect of my life I can never pursue beyond the choir stand." Lyriq shrugged.

"I think we need to find you a sponsor and a group here, babe. You're in California now, weed is legal, plentiful, and everywhere. And for you, it's a trigger. We need to get you in a group so you can learn to cope with its presence, as opposed to caving to its temptation."

"You act like I just told you I was about to smoke crack or something," Lyriq snapped.

"Whoa, wait a minute, babe. I'm not insinuating anything of the sort. I'm simply saying that we need to be proactive and find a narcotics anonymous group. We are operating as one now and I'm not trying to send you to a meeting alone. I want to stand strong with you, Lyriq."

She raised her hands in surrender. "You're right and I'm sorry. It's just that I didn't have these kinds of temptations at home. My world was small; work, home, and church. I sheltered myself from temptation, but I don't know if I can do that here. An innocent outing turned into a fight with the only friend I've made here," Lyriq confessed.

"Do you think she took you to the studio with malicious intent?"

Stacey Covington-Lee

"Absolutely not! Baily had the best of intentions, and I ran out like a child."

"I think you should call her, explain the situation and apologize if necessary. I'm sure she will understand," Ryker encouraged as he wrapped her in a comforting embrace.

"Thank you, love, you're the best. Now would you please feed me? You drove right past the diner without thinking of my poor stomach."

Ryker laughed. "Go change, greedy, and we'll go out for brunch."

CHAPTER 15

Lyriq asked Bailey to meet her at the corner café for a little heart-to-heart. Thankfully, Bailey agreed and Lyriq sat nervously waiting for her friend to arrive. She played the words she'd say to Bailey over and over in her head. She didn't want to be judged for past behavior or treated differently, like some kind of new-aged crack head. Lyriq didn't want past transgressions held against her, she wasn't that person anymore.

"Good morning, sweetheart, what are you in the mood for today?" Ms. Betty beamed down at Lyriq with a smile on her face.

"Good morning to you," Lyriq sang back. The kindness that radiated from Ms. Betty brought a calm to Lyriq, a sense of peace. "You're mighty happy today."

"God woke me up in my right mind, gave me another day, and my grandbaby is coming to spend a few days with me."

"Oh, that's wonderful. Hopefully, I'll get to meet him or her."

"Not likely, after today, I'll be on vacation for a bit. But maybe you'll meet her next time," Ms. Betty offered as a consolation prize of sorts. "So, what will you have?"

"A latte for now, please. I'm going to wait and order food with Bailey."

Ms. Betty surprised Lyriq by sliding into the booth across from her. "I know you're a grown woman, capable of making your own decisions, but please watch how much trust you put in this friendship between you and this Bailey. You two are from different worlds and her world has nothing nice to offer you."

"Are you being fair, Ms. Betty? You don't even know her."

"Trust me, I know her. I know her type. Just be cautious, sweetheart," Ms. Betty warned as she stood and sashayed off to get Lyriq's coffee. By the time she returned to the table, Bailey was there with a half-smile, half-smirk on her face. She knew the woman didn't like her, but she couldn't have cared less. Ms. Betty was no more than an annoyance to her.

"So, what's on your mind, Lyriq? Why did you call me here? After our last outing, I figured I wouldn't be hearing from you anymore."

Lyriq sighed deeply as the words she'd planned to say scurried away from her. Her past life wasn't something she was ready to fully disclose to Bailey, or anyone for that matter. As long as her husband was good with knowing who she was and who she is now, that's all that mattered. "I wanted to apologize. My behavior the other day was childish and totally uncalled for. I shouldn't have snapped on you the way that I did, and I am terribly sorry."

He Won't Go

After a shrug or two, Bailey accepted Lyriq's apology, but had to ask, "Why did you go off though? I mean, it was weed. You acted as though old boy offered you meth or something."

"Look, I'm from a small country town and every addict I know started out with smoking a little weed. That's always stayed with me, been in the forefront of my mind and I don't want to risk ever going down that addiction road." Lyriq knew there was so much truth left out of her explanation, but that's all Bailey would get for now.

Ms. Betty returned with delicious plates of food and a fresh latte for Lyriq. "Gee thanks, this water is good for me," Bailey chided sarcastically.

"Would you like something else to drink?" Ms. Betty asked with all the sincerity of a venomous snake.

"Yes, I would. I'll also have a latte," Bailey barked.

Ms. Betty huffed off as Lyriq shook her head. "How can you two dislike each other so much, when you don't know each other from Adam's house cat?"

"Adam's house cat? Don't bring those country behind saying out here. I don't ever want to hear about Adam or his cat again," Bailey snorted.

"Just wait, you'll learn to love my sayings."

Ms. Betty gently placed Bailey's coffee on the table and asked if they needed anything else. When they said no, she placed the bill on the table, winked at Lyriq, turned and walked away.

"Why is she winking like you're her girlfriend?"

"She's just happy, Bailey. She's taking a few days off to spend with her grandchild. I would be winking and happy too if a cherished loved one was coming to visit."

"I wonder if she's going to bring the little girl in here during her stay?"

"How did you know her grandchild is a girl?"

"Lucky guess…" Bailey's voice trailed off as she turned her head and focused on Ms. Betty.

"You okay?"

"Yeah, I'm good. What are you doing with the rest of your day?" Bailey asked as she slowly turned her attention away from Ms. Betty.

"With only a couple weeks left before school starts, I'd like to go do a little more shopping. You know, be prepared to wow my co-workers and those snotty nosed kids," Lyriq laughed hardily.

"You are so corny. Come on, I've got the afternoon off and wouldn't mind hitting L.A. again. But I do have to stop by the studio and grab something from Rogan. Do you mind waiting in the car for like five minutes when we get there?"

He Won't Go

"Not at all, but if it's ok with you, I'd like to go in and apologize to him for my behavior in the studio and at church."

"Church?"

"I'll tell you about it on the way," Lyriq sighed.

The ride into L.A. was filled with small talk. For whatever reason, Bailey never seemed willing to participate in deep conversation unless it was about anyone but her. So far, Lyriq had only learned the most basic of information about her new friend. No deep details about her family life, how she grew up, or why her most recent relationship ended. Somehow, she managed to glaze right over any questions that required an in-depth answer. They shopped a bit, Bailey avoided a couple more questions, they got a couple of frozen yogurts, and Bailey skirted a couple more questions. It made Lyriq replay Ms. Betty's warning over a few times in her head.

When they finally arrived at the studio, Bailey asked Lyriq if she was sure she was comfortable going in. Lyriq assured her she was, so they eased out the car and went in without knocking. The bloom of smoke that welcomed them was overwhelming. Lyriq wanted to turn tail and run again, but didn't want to be seen as some simple, naïve little girl again. She could feel her head start to swim a bit, but tried to reign herself back in. Rogan was inside with another rather large gentleman, who was covered in tattoos and flashing a beautiful pearly white smile at them. They were smoking weed and drinking cognac.

"Ladies, what a pleasant surprise. Come on in and join us," Rogan mumbled with a wave of his hand.

"Nah, I just stopped by to pick up that bag I left over here last week and Lyriq was just along for the ride," Bailey replied as she nodded in Lyriq's direction. She noticed Lyriq lightly swaying as the big dude continued to blow smoke in her direction. "Lyriq, step back closer to the door," Bailey barked out of concern.

"Leave your girl alone and let her enjoy the contact high," big dude laughed.

"No, she's not about that life," Bailey warned.

"Yeah man, she's a good church girl. Chill out and let her step away," Rogan added.

While Bailey stepped to a back room to retrieve her bag, Lyriq reluctantly took a couple of steps towards the door as she offered an apology to Rogan.

"Rogan, I'm sorry I freaked out on you here the other week and again in church. I guess the idea of getting high or being around drugs just freaks me out a bit."

"No worries, I totally understand. And if you ever want to do a little recording, let me know and I'll make sure the studio is available and substance free for you."

"Thanks, but I think I'll stick to singing in the choir stand," Lyriq chuckled.

He Won't Go

Bailey reappeared with her bag, gave Rogan a brief hug and headed towards the door where Lyriq was waiting. Before the ladies could make their escape, the big dude pushed himself out of the chair where he'd been resting and extended business cards in Lyriq's direction. "If you ever feel like partying, give me a call. I always keep that good-good on hand," he winked. Bailey snatched both cards, gave a dry "Thanks," and pushed Lyriq out the door.

As they got ready to drive away, Bailey tossed the two cards to the back of the car. "That guy is such a jerk, I don't know why Rogan lets him hang around."

Back in the studio, Rogan chastised his friend for offering his card to the ladies. "You heard me say she's a good church girl. You should've respected that and not offered the cards."

"Good church girl, my behind. Did you see how she was responding to the smoke, swaying? She might be a church girl now, but she was an addict before. Who knows, she could end up being my best customer."

"Man, I'm telling you, leave her alone! If by some crazy circumstance she calls you, still leave her alone. I mean it," Rogan warned.

The ladies drove off for more shopping and small talk. After another hour or so, they headed back towards Irvine. As they pulled to the front of the condo, Lyriq unbuckled her seat belt and reached in the back for her shopping bags. In the process, she noticed the big dude's cards and foolishly slid one into her bag before turning back around and bidding Bailey a good evening.

Bailey watched Lyriq waltz into her building before pulling off. She went up a couple of blocks and stopped in at the café. She stopped one of the waitresses and asked, "Is Ms. Betty still here?" When the woman advised that Betty had just left, Bailey cursed as she stormed out. "Where are you with my daughter, old lady?"

CHAPTER 16

"Hello"

"Hey babe, are you busy?"

"Hey, Ryker. No, I'm just waiting for my sweet husband to get home so we can start enjoying our last weekend before my job kicks in. Please don't tell me you're working late?"

"No, but I do need a favor. Meet me downstairs in front of the building," Ryker instructed.

"Now?"

"Yes, now! Come on down."

"Ugh, give me a second to put on some shoes and grab my keys." Lyriq, feeling slightly annoyed, did as she said she would and hustled out the door. It seemed to take the elevator a short lifetime to arrive, but a few seconds later, Lyriq was padding her way through the lobby and out the doors. To her great surprise, Ryker was standing beside a new black Porsche Panamera that was covered in a huge red bow.

"I can't have my baby walking home from school, can I?" Ryker smiled as he dangled the key fob in the air.

Lyriq squealed like a kid on Christmas morning. "Are you serious, babe, is this really mine?"

"It sure is. You so graciously gave your old car to the church when we moved up here, it seemed only fair to replace it with something better. I figured something sleek and sexy would look good wrapped around you."

"This is my dream car! Baby, thank you so much. Let me get my license so we can take it for a spin." Lyriq jetted back into the building before Ryker could even reply. He stood there grinning, completely pleased with himself that he was able to make his wife so happy.

The spin in the car turned into an hour drive and a stop for dinner. Lyriq was still on cloud nine as she whipped through the city. She even went so far as to name the car Midnight, saying it was her other beautiful, black man. When they finally made it back home, Ryker said he wanted to go wash the day off of himself. After he'd stepped into the shower, Lyriq stripped off her clothes and decided to join him. She wanted to show her husband how appreciative she was for her new ride. Ryker closed his eyes as she stepped in behind him and rubbed her hands over his shoulders. His heart rate increased when she started kissing his neck and moved her slippery, soapy hands all over his body. She moved to the front of him and kissed him deeply as the water rained down on them. He could hardly take it when she knelt to pleasure him. When she stood back up, he lifted her, she wrapped her legs around his waist, and he steadied her against the shower wall. She moaned when he entered her and tears, mixing with the water, streamed down her cheeks as he made her orgasm over and over again. He shook as his body released, unable to hold out any longer. He held her as she gently slid down his body, they stepped out and allowed their wet bodies to collapse in a tangled heap onto the bed.

Ryker was in the kitchen cooking breakfast while Lyriq was unpacking her shopping bags from the previous day and showing Ryker all the cute clothes she'd purchased for school. He teased her, saying she was more anxious than the students. He was laughing at his jokes when he turned to find her gazing at a business card.

"What's that, babe?" He asked.

"Nothing, just a card from a street hustler selling CD's, as if people still listen to those things," she snorted as she tossed the card on the table.

"Sounds like old boy needs to get a new hustle," Ryker replied as he placed their plates on the table. He went back to the counter to grab their mugs of coffee. He sat down with the expectation of looking at the business card, but it was no longer on the table. He shrugged figuring she'd tossed the card in the trash.

"So, what's on the agenda for the day? Please don't tell me you have to work. It's the last Saturday I'll have that won't be consumed with grading papers and uploading test scores," Lyriq whined with puppy dog eyes.

"Come on, babe, don't look at me like that. I promise I'll only be there for a little while, no more than four hours and then I'm all yours. We can go and hang out in L.A, grab dinner at a swanky restaurant, whatever you want to do," he said, reaching for her hand. "I promise, just four hours, okay?"

"Fine," she relented through clenched teeth.

They finished breakfast and as Ryker prepared to go into the office, Lyriq began to clean the condo. She started in the kitchen and before she could finish with the dishes and wipe everything down, Ryker appeared in a crisp white dress shirt, dark jeans, and loafers. He looked and smelled delightful. After a gentle peck on the lips and a promise to return shortly, he was out the door. Lyriq finished the kitchen and went to put her new clothes in the bedroom closet. As soon as she went in the first bag, there it was...that card. Why hadn't she just thrown it away? She picked it up and eyeballed the card for a few seconds before tossing it on the bed. Again, she admired her purchases before hanging them neatly in the closet. After folding the bags for the trash, she decided to change the bed sheets. She snatched up the card, took another look at it and placed it on the nightstand before ripping the sheets from the bed. She padded off to the laundry room and threw the sheets in the wash. With a quick stop by the linen closet to grab fresh sheets, she started stretching them over the corners of the mattress. After what seemed like a short eternity of wrestling with the bed, it was beautifully made. She went to start cleaning the bathrooms, but as if it had its own gravitational pull, she returned to the card from big dude. Lyriq twirled it in her fingers and then swiftly snatched up her phone. Like a possessed woman, she dialed his number.

"Hello?"

"Umm, this is Lyriq. I met you in the studio the other day."

"I remember you, the church girl. What can I do for you?"

"I was just wondering if I could buy some weed from you?"

"Church girl, there are dispensaries everywhere, you don't need me for weed."

"You're right, I don't need you," Lyriq blurted and ended the call.

The phone rang right back, and she could see it was big dude's number. She took a deep breath and tried to muster the strength not to answer. She called The Lord's name on the third ring and answered on the fourth.

"Why are you calling me? You said I didn't need you and you're right."

"Because we both know you can't find weed like mine in a store. Where are you? I can bring you a blunt. This first one will be on the house," he offered. He knew if he could get her to take it, he'd have a customer for life.

"I'm in Irvine, but I can ride to L.A. real quick," Lyriq said as a single tear journeyed down her cheek. She knew she was treading dangerous waters.

"I wouldn't put you out like that. I'll meet you in an hour at the park. There's a gazebo by the lake, I'll see you there," big dude instructed and disconnected the call.

Lyriq checked the time, she had three hours and fifteen minutes before Ryker would return. She jumped in the shower and threw on some leggings and a tee shirt and shot out the door. She arrived at the park twenty minutes early and sat there trying to convince herself to leave. She grabbed her phone and dialed her Narcotics Anonymous sponsor back home. The phone rang and eventually went to voicemail. She thought about calling her mom, but she'd end up telling someone about Lyriq's dilemma and the news would weave its way back to Constance, and that's the last thing she needed. Everyone knew Constance was just waiting for Lyriq to backslide so she could convince Ryker to file for divorce. So, Lyriq took a deep breath instead of dialing another number, and tossed the phone back in her purse. It wasn't long before a Bentley pulled up beside her and big dude looked over with a silly grin plastered across his face. They both exited their cars and took a seat under the gazebo.

"Nice new ride you got there, church girl," big dude said with a nod towards her car.

"Thanks. It's a gift from my husband," Lyriq mumbled.

"Well, here's another gift for you," he said as he passed her a neatly rolled blunt. "You've never had anything this good," he smirked. He held it out for Lyriq to take and watched her slowly reach for it as if it were a snake that might strike if she got too close.

118

He Won't Go

"Why are you being so generous?"

"Church girl, I saw how you inhaled and swayed with the smoke in the studio. I could tell you'd smoked before, and I just want you to know it's ok. Weed is a natural herb, and you don't have to be ashamed about partaking. I figured you'd never actually go to a dispensary, so this is me being a nice guy."

"Anyone ever tell you you're a fast talker? My dad told me never to trust a fast talker.," Lyriq said doubtfully.

"Hey, I'm just trying to be nice. I'm not selling any used cars, no need for me to be slick or a so-called fast talker."

"You know what, let me just pay you for this," Lyriq offered. "I don't like being indebted to anyone."

Big dude stood to his feet and stuffed his hands in his pockets. "You owe me nothing. You're indebted to me for nothing. Enjoy," he smiled before ambling off to his car.

Lyriq sat for a moment longer. She placed the blunt under her nose and inhaled deeply. The aroma instantly took her back to days gone by. Dark days, troubled days. But those days also brought her ecstasy…before they brought the storm. She now had to decide what she wanted more, that feeling of ecstasy or her new life. She could not have both

.

CHAPTER 17

Bailey had been calling Lyriq incessantly for the past two hours. Since learning her daughter was in town, she'd become obsessed with finding out where she and her wretched grandmother, Betty, were staying. Hoping Lyriq could provide some insight, since she was so close with the old bat, Bailey began to call Lyriq's cell. Now, out of desperation, Bailey decided to drive over to the condo in hopes of catching Lyriq at home. Bailey jumped off the elevator and went to knock on the door, but the door was cracked. Bailey pushed it open a little further, just enough to poke her head in.

"Hello, is anyone home? You here, Lyriq?"

Bailey stood still, listening for voices or any sound for that matter. When she didn't hear anyone respond, she took a step into the condo and called out again, this time louder and more authoritative. "Lyriq, you home?" After a couple of seconds, she heard what sounded like a muffled groan, but not the pleasurable kind. Again, she bellowed, "Lyriq, you here?" Again, she heard a faint groan. She started stepping towards the bedroom when she noticed the balcony door ajar. Bailey pushed the door open to see Lyriq half draped across a lounge chair. Her arms flopped over her head, which was almost resting on the ground and a half-burned blunt, one of the fattest Bailey had ever seen, lay beside an emptied glass of red wine. *Where in the world was Ryker*, Bailey thought to herself, *and how had Lyriq let this happen?*

Standing over Lyriq, Bailey reached down and snatched her friend up by the collar. "Wake up, Lyriq, wake up," she barked as she shook Lyriq back and forth like a rag doll. "What have you done and where is Ryker?" Bailey questioned as she shook and lightly smacked Lyriq's face. "Wake up, girl, wake up," Bailey barked as she laid a more stinging smack to Lyriq's cheek.

Lyriq groaned and slurred her words as she feebly tried to push Bailey away. "Stop hitting me, leave me alone…" her weak speech trailing off into nothingness.

"Tell me where Ryker is and I'll leave you alone," Bailey almost shouted directly into her ear.

This new tactic seemed to have worked. With the mention of her husband's name, Lyriq's eyes fluttered open. First bringing Bailey into focus and then slowly looking about her. And there it was, her eyes landed on the wine glass and half-smoked blunt. Her eyes welled up with tears.

"What time is it?" Lyriq slurred.

"It's twelve-thirty and you clearly couldn't wait to get the party started."

"Oh no, Ryker is supposed to be home by one o'clock. Oh God, how did I let this happen?" She whimpered as she attempted, unsuccessfully, to get up. "Bailey, please help me up. I've got to get myself together before Ryker gets home."

"That's going to take a miracle," Bailey huffed.

"You can punish me later, Bailey, but right now I need you to help me," Lyriq practically begged.

With anger etched across her face and a string of expletives escaping her lips, Bailey dragged Lyriq to the master bath and started running an ice-cold shower. She practically ripped the clothes from Lyriq's body and stood her under the waterfall of freezing water. Lyriq jumped and screeched like a tortured cat. She tried to scramble out of the shower, but Bailey forced her back under the cascading water.

"If you're bad enough to smoke that poison and drink that liquor, then you're bad enough to stand under this water."

Once she was satisfied that Lyriq was alert and able to stand under her own weight, Bailey shut the water off and gave her a towel. "Here, dry yourself off and step out. You need to hurry and brush your teeth, your mouth smells like a freaking trash dumpster. I don't know what you're going to do about those bloodshot eyes," she fussed as she rummaged through the medicine cabinet, looking for Visine.

With a mouth full of toothpaste, Lyriq asked Bailey to go clean her mess up from the balcony. Bailey did as she was asked and picked up the empty wine glass and the remainder of the blunt. Not seeing the small square of tin foil that held ashes from the marijuana, Bailey went back in, washed the wine glass, returned it to the cabinet and headed for the bathroom with what remained of the blunt. She lifted the lid to the toilet when Lyriq called out in an almost panicked voice.

"Wait, what are you doing with that?" Lyriq questioned.

"I'm going to flush it. Your party is over! Do you hear me, your little party is over, Lyriq!" Bailey barked as she dropped the marijuana cigarette in the toilet and flushed it. She looked back at Lyriq who looked as if she wanted to dive in the toilet to retrieve her poison. Disgust filled Bailey's spirit and Lyriq could see it all over her friend's face. Tears filled Lyriq's eyes as she backed away.

Stumbling into the bedroom, Lyriq slipped into her bathrobe and tied it tightly around her waist. She tried to hide herself in it. She felt ashamed and embarrassed to have Bailey look at her with disappointed eyes. She felt her friend's gaze burning a hole in her back but before she could turn around and offer an explanation, she heard Ryker coming through the front door. Panic filled her eyes and she looked at Bailey as if to say, "What do I do?'

Bailey dashed over to Lyriq, put her arm around Lyriq's waist and whispered, "Lean on me and play along." Ryker entered the room in time to see Bailey holding his wife and helping her into bed. He heard Bailey speak gently, "Okay girl, your man is home now. He'll take great care of you."

With an extended hand and a warm smile, Bailey approached Ryker. "Hello, I'm Bailey, Lyriq's friend."

With a twinge of concern and confusion, Ryker took her hand in his and gave it a polite shake. Hello Bailey, I'm Ryker, it's nice to finally put a face with a name." He released her hand and looked between the two women. "What's going on here, is my bride okay?"

"I think she'll be fine. We were talking on the phone when she started feeling queasy and I heard her lose her stomach. I got concerned and decided to come check on her. I'm not sure what you guys had for breakfast, but whatever it was it didn't agree with Lyriq. I think with a little rest and seltzer water, she'll be fine."

"Is that your professional opinion?" Ryker chuckled lightly as he made his way to Lyriq's bedside.

Giggling bashfully, Bailey replied, "Yes, but my bill will reflect much more." She stepped towards the bedroom door and told Ryker to take care of his wife and she'd check in later. A few seconds later, they heard the front door close. Bailey left Lyriq to fill in any other lies required to cover up her foolish, drug driven decisions.

CHAPTER 18

Bailey put finding her daughter on the back burner for the moment. Right now, she had to deal with the devil that was attacking her friend. She exited Lyriq's building, jumped in her car, and headed straight for L.A. She whipped into the studio parking lot and burst through the door, startling Rogan.

"Girl, why are you bursting through here like you're the cops? Got me wondering what crime I committed," Rogan huffed in annoyance.

"Have you seen Bishop?" Bailey asked with venom in her voice.

"Nah, his big behind hasn't been in here today. Why? He's the last person I'd expect you to be looking for."

"Rogan, why do you continue to let him hang out here? You know he's nothing but trouble. Somehow his fat butt managed to get to Lyriq. I found her this morning stoned out of her mind," Bailey said tearfully as she flopped on the small couch.

"You mean the lady who was in here apologizing?"

"Yes! I know he got to her somehow, Rogan. When I found her, she was gone and half of his signature blunt was lying beside her.

We both know when he gets his sights set on someone new, he laces his weed. She got far more than just marijuana."

"I told him my studio is not his hunting ground. I also told him to leave her alone. Are you sure it was him?"

"I told you, I saw the blunt. Plus, she's new here, she wouldn't even know where else to get that stuff."

"Think she's going to be okay?"

"She's got secrets like everyone else, so only God knows. But I need you to help me keep Bishop away from her...please!"

~~~

Ryker stood over Lyriq, gently brushing the wet curls from her face. He looked lovingly down at her, caressing her face. "Baby, what do you need? What can I do to help you feel better?"

Lyriq turned her head towards Ryker and opened her eyes. He instantly snatched his hand from her and stepped back. For a second, it was his father's drug-induced eyes looking up at him. He shuddered and stepped further away from the bed. Leaning against the dresser, he took a few deep breaths to collect himself.

"Babe, are you okay?" Lyriq quizzed. When Ryker didn't respond, she swung her legs over the side of the bed and stood to walk towards him, but her walk was more of a drunken stumble. "What's wrong, Babe, are you feeling sick too?"

He Won't Go

"What's wrong with you, Lyriq and don't you lie to me," Ryker asked with eyes as cold as ice.

"Bailey was right, it must've been something I ate. My stomach is terribly upset," she explained, averting her eyes from his. After a few seconds, she leaned in to hug him, but stumbled back when he pushed her away. "Ryker, what is wrong with you? Why would you push me like that?"

"Why would you lie to me, Lyriq? Do you think I'm some naive country boy that don't know what the hell is going on? I told you not to lie to me," he barked. "What's wrong with you?"

Lyriq jumped at the harshness of his tone and begin to cry softly. "Ryker, I'm so sorry. Baby, I didn't mean for it happen. I thought I'd just have a little…" Her voice trailed off as she flopped on the bed and sobbed, ashamed of what she'd done, too embarrassed to look at her husband.

"You've got five minutes to get yourself together," Ryker barked before leaving the room.

"Oh God, Ryker are you putting me out? Please no, I'm sorry," she sobbed.

"I'm not putting you out, but we need to leave," he explained in a voice devoid of love or concern. He continued out the room as he dialed a number on his phone.

"Hello?"

Stacey Covington-Lee

Lyriq strained to hear her husband's phone conversation, to try and gain some idea about where they were going, but he'd moved too far into the front of the condo. She couldn't hear anything above a murmur.

"Pastor Carlton, I'm so sorry to bother you with business on your personal time, but I need to meet with you ASAP in your office. Would that be possible?" Ryker asked as he tried to keep his anger from being audible.

"Must be serious, you're addressing me as Pastor instead of friend. I'm already at the church and will be waiting in my office."

"Thanks, I'll see you shortly," Ryker replied tersely before disconnecting the call. He turned around to bellow for Lyriq, but stopped short when she appeared in the doorway dressed in athletic gear and sneakers.

"If you give me more time, I can dress in something more acceptable," she mumbled.

"We don't have more time, let's go."

Ryker ushered her out the building and into the car. They rode in complete silence, but when he turned on the road to the church, Lyriq broke the silence with panicked pleas.

"You can't be serious? Why are we coming here, Ryker? Am I supposed to confess my sins and beg your forgiveness? I'm not even dressed appropriately enough to enter the sanctuary. Please, take me

128

back home, let me get myself together before making me face these church folks."

"You're not facing a bunch of church folks. We've got a meeting with Pastor Carlton. We need some intervention right now; we need to face this demon and find a way to defeat it now, before it becomes too big."

"So, I'm a demon now?" Lyriq huffed like a child.

"Don't do that, Lyriq, don't twist my words or my intent. I'm trying to be a good man, a good husband and stand in battle with my wife."

She didn't think it was possible, but his response to her outburst made her feel even smaller than she already did. She decided that now was the time to put on her big girl panties and accept the help and support her man was offering. As she unbuckled her seat belt and stepped past the car door being held open by Ryker, she mumbled softly, "I'm sorry." Without response, he took her hand and walked with her into the church offices.

Pastor Carlton appeared in the doorway of his office and greeted them both with a warm embrace. He then stepped to the side and extended his hand into his office, inviting them to step in and have a seat. He observed Ryker's tense jawline and Lyriq's sullen eyes. He couldn't imagine what could've gone so wrong this early in their marriage. He cleared his head of any preconceived notions and gave a quick, silent prayer to be a help to this obviously troubled couple.

"So, tell me, how can I be of service to you two?" Pastor Carlton asked straight-faced.

"Pastor, when I called you and told you of our relationship and my intent to marry my beautiful bride, what I didn't share was that she is a recovering addict. Lyriq here has been doing so well and has even secured herself a teaching job at a school neat the house. I don't know the details of how it happened, but somehow during the course of the last few hours, my wife fell off the wagon. I wanted to come here so that I can, hopefully, find out the truth about how this relapse occurred and the best way for us get control of the situation before it gets too out of hand."

Lyriq looked between the two men, trying to decide how close their relationship was. She knew nothing about Ryker discussing her, or their relationship, with this man before now.

Pastor Carlton's eyes softened as they fell to Lyriq. "Ma'am, I know this is awkward and probably feels a little intimidating to be meeting with me like this. I saw you all in church last Sunday but didn't get a chance to have as proper an introduction as I'd have liked. I have known Ryker for quite some time, I consider him a great friend of mine. But I want to assure you this is a judge-free zone. The only side I will ever take is the side of truth. You can speak freely, and your words will never leave these four walls."

Lyriq closed her eyes and breathed deeply. Something told her she could trust this man, that he would somehow understand her situation better than her husband ever could. She opened her eyes and recounted how they were smoking in the studio, how big dude gave her his card, and how she'd called him after Ryker left for work. She tried to explain the lure of the card, or maybe it was the lure of what the card represented…the high. She explained how big dude gave her the marijuana for free and she smoked it like a fool. Tears of regret and self-loathing streamed down her face.

The pastor exhaled. "In your heart, you knew it wasn't free. It never is. The *free* one is to get you hooked. He probably had it laced with cocaine or something. He's a dealer and his job is to get you hooked and bleed you dry. I know this because I was first a dealer and then an addict. I was the fool that started smoking up his own product."

Lyriq's eyes almost bulged out of her head. She couldn't believe what she was hearing. She looked to Ryker to see if he was just as shocked, but he sat there as if he'd heard nothing, or at least nothing new.

"Yes, your husband already knows. After hearing of my story, it was his generosity that allowed us to start the community outreach program that helps recovering addicts to get their lives back on track. He knows that overcoming is possible. Through our program, he's witnessed many success stories over the past couple of years."

"But I've also witnessed tragedy," Ryker interjected as he turned to face Lyriq. "I've witnessed people fall and never get up. I've held the hand of the mother who lost her son to drugs. You know how I lost my father. I can't live through that again, baby. I need you to commit to joining this program and allowing Pastor Carlton to be your sponsor. You have to commit to that right here, right now, or I'm out. I will not stand by and watch you fall deeper into the trappings of this demon. The choice is yours."

CHAPTER 19

Lyriq was relieved and proud to have successfully made it through her first week of school. She'd gotten acquainted with her student's parents, built a great rapport with the kids and fellow faculty member, and most importantly, attended two Narcotics Anonymous meetings at the church. She couldn't have asked for the week to have gone any better. Now getting home and freshened up for her date with Ryker was all she was focused on. As she jumped into the car to head home, her phone rang, and the screen displayed Bailey's cute face. Lyriq had managed to avoid her for the past week and still wasn't quite ready to face her. Lyriq threw the car in reverse and backed out of her parking spot. As she rolled down the street and past the park, she noticed big dude's Bentley parked near the gazebo where she'd met him. Her mind raced as she wondered what he was doing back in her area of town. Was he looking for her or just another weak, gullible person to push his poison to? When the phone rang again, she mindlessly pushed the talk button on her steering wheel and cursed herself when Bailey's voice came booming through the speakers.

"Clearly, you're still alive, so why haven't you been answering my calls?"

"I'm sorry, Bailey," Lyriq offered as the park shrank away in her rearview mirror. "Honestly, I was too embarrassed to face

133

anyone, especially you. I'd never imagined you'd see me in such a state. I can only imagine what you must think of me."

"You're human, Lyriq, and as friends we're supposed to trust one another with our good and our bad. Are we not friends?"

"Of course we are, but geez, two minutes into this friendship and you're having to save me from myself."

"Trust me, you'll have a chance to pay me back. My life is in shambles, and I will surely need saving sooner rather than later," Bailey chuckled.

"I look forward to it." Lyriq smiled.

"Hey, do you have a few minutes to chat? I'm sitting here at the corner café."

Lyriq glanced at the clock and shrugged. "I guess I could meet for a couple of minutes, but just a couple. I've got to get home and freshen up for my dinner date with Ryker tonight."

"I promise not to hold you."

Lyriq opened the door to the café and perused the tables and booths looking for the familiar face of her only California friend. After a few seconds, her eyes landed on Bailey, who was preoccupied with her cell phone. She didn't realize Lyriq had arrived until she was literally sitting across from her, clearing her throat.

"Hey girl, I didn't see you walk in, but thank you so much for coming."

He Won't Go

"No problem. What's going on with you? You seem really distracted by that phone," Lyriq remarked with a nod towards Bailey's hands.

"Oh, this is nothing," Bailey assured as she placed the phone face down on the table. "But I do need your help with something."

A slim, blonde waitress approached the table. "Can I get you ladies something to drink?"

"Nothing for me," Lyriq answered.

"Iced cappuccino," Bailey responded without looking up at the woman. Once the waitress sauntered off, Bailey continued with her request. "Do you feel close enough to Betty to ask her a few questions about her granddaughter?"

"You mean Ms. Betty who works here?"

"Yes, the old witch that looks at me with contempt every time I roll up in here."

"Why would you want to know anything about her grandchild? For some reason, you two can't stand each other, so I can't fathom why you would want to know anything about her or her family," Lyriq questioned.

"Because her grandchild is my daughter," Bailey answered very matter-of-factly. "And I need to see my baby. My mother has custody but allows Betty to also spend time with her. Betty is my child's father's mother. The two grandmothers have refused me

135

access to my baby girl. I figured if you casually asked Betty where she lives and how long my little girl will be visiting with her, then I could pop up at her house and catch a glimpse of my baby."

The skinny waitress placed the cappuccino in front of Bailey but was shooed away before she could ask about a food order.

Lyriq sat there with her mouth gaped open, in a total state of shock. She remembered Ms. Betty making a comment about Bailey not being the kind of person she needed to associate with, but she just thought Ms. Betty was picking up some weird vibe. Lyriq never imagined that the two women had a connection, let alone a blood connection. Lyriq rubbed her head, trying to gather her thoughts. Finally finding her words, she asked, "Why not just ask your child's father about arranging a meeting?"

"No! I can't allow him back into my life in any way. If we happen to run into one another, I act as if he's a stranger. He's a very bad man, Lyriq, and regardless of how much she tries to deny it, even Ms. Betty knows that. I'm sure he doesn't even realize my little girl is in town."

Again, Lyriq rubbed her head, trying to make sense of it all. "How would I even question Ms. Betty? She's on vacation and I don't have any of her contact information. I don't even know her last name, let alone her address. I wish I could help you, Bailey, but I just don't know how."

He Won't Go

The skinny waitress walked back over to ask if she could get them anything else. Her eyes bulged when Bailey slid a crisp one-hundred-dollar bill in her direction and told her it was hers if she'd provide her with Ms. Betty's phone number or address. The waitress looked around to see who was watching. She turned her eyes back to the bill and looked at it as if she were staring at a T-bone steak. Temptation gripped the woman, but then her common sense and loyalty prevailed.

"God knows I wish I could help you with that, ma'am, but I just can't, and I can assure you that no one here will give you that kind of information. Just put your money away and if you ask another server, management will ban you from the café," the woman warned before leaving to check on her other tables.

"What the hell kind of hold does that old woman have on this place that no one will say anything about her? I know that broke chick could've used this," Bailey huffed as she waved the hundred-dollar bill through the air. Frustration getting the best of her, Bailey dropped her head in her hands, "I just want to see my baby."

Lyriq reached across the table and caressed Bailey's hand. She wanted to comfort her friend, but she mostly wanted to know why both the baby's grandparents were withholding her from her mother. What could Bailey have possibly done that would warrant them keeping her from her child? Lyriq cleared her throat and worked up the nerve to toss out a couple of questions.

Stacey Covington-Lee

"If you don't mind my asking, how was your mom able to take custody of your daughter? I mean, how can they legally keep you from your child?"

"When I met my baby's father I was in a really bad place. He presented himself as a good guy who was willing to help me out, but instead he was an abusive monster that forced me to do really ugly things. When I finally broke away from him, I was pregnant and destitute. My mom let me back in the house long enough to give birth. She told me once I could provide a safe, healthy environment for my baby, she'd give her back to me. She put me out the house and I've been busting my butt with odd jobs trying to save enough and prove that I can be a fit parent. Leaving my baby was my only option. Otherwise, she'd have ended up in the system and I couldn't let that happen."

"I'm so sorry, Bailey, I had no idea. God knows I wish there were something I could do to help, but I'm clueless as to how."

"I know... I knew it was a long shot, but I had to ask you. Look, I know you've got plans with hubby, so go on home and I'm going to head out too. I've got to pick up a client and she's a big tipper, so I can't be late."

"Okay, but you're sure you're going to be all right?"

"Of course," Bailey said as she tossed a ten-dollar bill on the table, stood and hugged Lyriq goodbye.

138

CHAPTER 20

Just as Lyriq finished her make-up, Ryker practically burst through the front door. He entered the bedroom and was already halfway out of his clothes. "I'm sorry I'm running late, babe," he said breathlessly as he planted a quick kiss on Lyriq's lips. "And I hope you don't mind, but Kane and Mona are meeting us at the restaurant."

"That's fine with me," Lyriq replied. "I haven't seen Mona since Vegas."

Ryker stepped from the shower, quickly wiped down and pulled on his boxer briefs. He looked up as he rubbed lotion over his thick body and caught Lyriq's gaze. She devoured him with her eyes, and it was all he could do to keep from snatching her up, pinning her to the wall, and having his way with her over and over again.

"You know, we can skip this dinner," he offered with lover's eyes.

"We could, but we've already cancelled on them once. And at the last minute, what will they think?"

"Who cares what they think," Ryker asserted as he eased up to her and nibbled at her ear and kissed on her neck.

Lyriq reluctantly pushed him away. "We can't be rude. We just know to hurry and eat and keep the conversation short, so we can get back and I can ride you until daybreak."

Ryker groaned seductively, "You promise?"

"I promise. Now hurry up."

The restaurant hostess advised Ryker and Lyriq that their dining companions had already arrived and then she proceeded to escort them to the table where Kane and Mona were patiently waiting. The couple stood to greet their tardy friends with smiles and open arms.

"We're so sorry to have kept you all waiting, but this one was running late from the office," Lyriq offered as she playfully nudged Ryker in the arm.

"Oh please, we haven't been here long at all. It's good to see you guys," Mona replied sweetly.

The maître d' approached the table and welcomed the new arrivals. He told them of the night's specials and made recommendations from their extensive wine list.

The couples opted for a bottle of sparkling cider for the table, thanked the maître d', and dove right into conversation about their day and the progress the guys were making on their firm's latest big project. It wasn't long before a waiter arrived with the cider. As he poured, he asked if anyone had any questions about the menu. Everyone was sure of what they wanted and ordered quickly so they could return to their conversation.

He Won't Go

While Kane and Ryker chattered away about business, Mona leaned in and asked, "Tell me, Lyriq, how was your first week in the classroom?"

"Honestly, Mona, it couldn't have gone any better. Ninety percent of the parents have assured me they'll be actively involved and none of the kids have misbehaved, not yet anyway. It's the first week so I know some of their behaviors will evolve into something that won't be as pleasant as they've been thus far. But enough about that, how is your candle business going?"

In her signature scruffy voice, Mona replied, "Things are going great! I've added several more upscale boutiques to my client list and am in the process of looking for retail space."

"That's amazing. I'm so happy…" Lyriq's words trailed off as she spotted Ms. Betty walking up the aisle near their table with a tall, chiseled man who was carrying a beautiful, curly-headed little girl in his arms.

When the trio got close enough, Lyriq stood and softly called out, "Ms. Betty, is that you?"

Ms. Betty stopped and so did her companion. "Well, hello. I didn't expect to see anyone from the café here," she nervously replied while motioning as if to say this place was too upscale for her café folks.

Stacey Covington-Lee

"Oh, I'm sorry, I didn't mean to intrude on your personal time," Lyriq said as she took her seat. She felt a little wounded by Ms. Betty's cool reaction to seeing her.

"Please forgive my rudeness, we're just anxious to get my granddaughter home and in bed. You understand." Ms. Betty nodded towards the table at large. "Good night," she added as they walked away.

"That was a little weird, honey," Ryker commented.

"Tell me about it. Ms. Betty is a waitress at the neighborhood café I frequent and she's normally so nice and welcoming. I mean, welcoming far beyond what her job requires. I don't understand why she was so curt tonight."

"I agree, Ms. Betty is a really nice lady, but that jackass with her is a piece of work," Kane added.

Confusion etched across her face, Lyriq asked, "Kane, how do you know Ms. Betty? From the café?"

"No, from my father. He had a relationship with her while he was with my mom. Their little affair produced that drug slinging, woman abusing, goon she was with. I can't even believe Ms. Betty let him near her grandbaby. But since he's the father, I guess she didn't have much choice."

Lyriq's mouth was gapped open. *That's the monster that abused Bailey and that was her little girl.* Feeling Ryker's hand on her arm, Lyriq snapped out her temporary shock.

142

He Won't Go

"Baby, you never told me you had a brother," Mona whined.

"We may share a bloodline, but he's no brother of mine. He's a thug and I have no doubt you'll see him on the six o'clock news one day for killing someone or being killed. He's an absolute trash human being."

With that comment, everyone backed away from the topic of Kane's brother, Craig Garrison, and welcomed the scrumptious food being placed in front of them. They ate, drank, and laughed, but Lyriq's mind never stopped whirling. Would she tell Bailey she saw her daughter? Without knowing how to locate Ms. Betty, what would be the point?

~~~

They'd barely made it in the door before Ryker pulled Lyriq into him and began kissing her ferociously. With her promises of sexual delight playing in his head all evening, Ryker was anxious to taste his wife, to have her wetness envelop him. He was not disappointed. Lyriq pulled out all the tricks, some he didn't know she had, but it was when she flipped over on top of him and began to ride him as if she were a jockey and he her racehorse that Ryker lost it. Each time she dropped down on his strength, she squeezed her walls, gripping and releasing until he could take no more. When she knew she'd gotten every drop he had to offer, she collapsed breathlessly onto his chest.

Stacey Covington-Lee

Lyriq woke up Saturday morning to the smell of freshly brewed coffee and sizzling bacon. She rubbed the sleep from her eyes as she eased out of bed. She padded her way to the kitchen to see Ryker placing scrambled eggs on plates and pouring coffee into mugs.

"Did you seriously get up and prepare breakfast?" She smiled.

"Oh, you earned this breakfast, baby. What else would you like, because you earned that too," he joked as he hopped around as if riding a pony.

"I see you've got jokes this morning," Lyriq laughed with him.

"I'm just saying that last night was amazing, but sex aside, I love you enough to give you whatever you think will make you happy."

"I have everything right here," she confirmed as she squeezed his hand. "You're all I need, you're my happiness, babe."

Ryker blessed the food and as they began to eat, he asked how she'd like to spend the day. Lyriq hesitated before telling Ryker about the conversation she'd had the day before with Bailey. She explained why she was so freaked out about seeing Ms. Betty, her son, and grandchild. She told him what a monster Bailey had said her baby's father was, and how Kane's comments about his brother confirmed everything Bailey had told her.

"The only thing that varied from what Bailey told me was that Ms. Betty was out with her son. According to Bailey, Ms. Betty had nothing to do with him and neither grandparent allowed him to see the little girl. I wonder what changed?" Lyriq questioned.

"Sweetheart, I think it's best for you to steer clear of all of it. Your plate is already full with us, work, and your sobriety, you don't need to add their drama. So, back to my question, what do you want to do today?"

"I'll stay out of it, but I did promise Bailey we'd have a late lunch today," Lyriq lied. "After that, I'd love for us to catch a movie."

Ryker looked at her doubtfully but agreed to the movie. "Fine, but stay out of their drama, Lyriq. I'm warning you."

Lyriq put her hands up in surrender. "No drama, babe, no drama."

"Fine, I'm going to get cleaned up and head to the office for a few hours. Call me and let me know what time I need to be back to get you for the movie."

CHAPTER 21

By four o'clock, Ryker hadn't heard from Lyriq. He signed off his computer and grabbed his cell. He used his handsome face to unlock the phone and touched the screen to call his wife. He was surprised when his call went to voicemail. Ryker dialed two more times and got the same result. Annoyance and concern were starting to brew deep inside of him. This was unlike Lyriq and the last thing she promised was no drama. He tried her number one more time, but this time there was an answer. Only problem was it wasn't his wife that answered.

"Who is this?" he huffed.

"Hi Ryker, it's Bailey. Lyriq is in the bathroom, but I'll have her call you when she comes out. Might be a minute though, her stomach is torn up."

"Are you all at the condo?"

"No, she's at my apartment, but she'll be home soon enough. She'll call you when she's on her way. Goodbye." And with that, Bailey disconnected the call.

Ryker immediately called Lyriq's number again, but there was no answer. Everything about Bailey, the way she was talking, what she said set off alarms for Ryker. He didn't know how, but he knew he had to find his wife. There was no way he could sit and wait for her to show up. He grabbed his satchel and made a run for the door.

"What's the hurry, man?" Kane asked as Ryker nearly bowled him over in the hallway.

"My bad. There's something up with Lyriq and I've got to try and find her."

"Find her? Did she get lost driving around, or was she in an accident or something? Do you need me to call the cops?" Kane quizzed.

"Nah man, she's somewhere with this friend of hers and I've got a really bad feeling about it. She won't take my call and the chick she's with finally answered and gave me some BS story about Lyriq being in the bathroom."

"What can I do to help, Ryker?"

"Say a prayer that my wife hasn't done anything stupid and that she's okay," Ryker requested as he dashed out the door.

After driving around the city for an hour and a half, hoping to spot her car and calling her incessantly, Ryker decided to stop by the condo in case she'd decided to head home. To his dismay, she still hadn't made it home. He tried her phone a few more times, but now it wasn't even ringing, it was going straight to voicemail. *Had it been turned off or had he been blocked?* Either way, he was growing angrier and more worried by the second. Then he decided he'd try the church. Maybe, by some miracle, she was at the church participating in a NA meeting.

Pulling up to the church, Ryker scanned the parking lot. He didn't see Lyriq's car, but maybe she'd just left or maybe she'd reached out to Pastor Carlton. He dashed into the church where he heard the youth choir practicing for Sunday service. There were a few other people milling around and as he turned to head down the hall towards Pastor Carlton's office, he bumped into Deacon Roosevelt, a dedicated church member who'd been instrumental in building Victory Land. He was also credited with helping to bring Pastor Carlton on board after the passing of their previous minister. He was a tall man with kind eyes that sparkled with flecks of gray. He had a salt and pepper goatee and was always quick to offer a handshake and a kind word.

"Slow down there, son. I'm an old man, if you mow me over, I may not be able to get back up," Deacon Roosevelt joked.

"I'm so sorry, Deacon. I didn't hurt you, did I?" Ryker teased back and tried to offer a sincere smile.

"Oh no, but what's your hurry, anything I can help you with?"

"I was just looking for Pastor Carlton. I wanted to see if he'd seen or spoken with my wife today."

"If he has, he didn't see or speak to her here. He hasn't been in today. He did call and have me message the regular NA attendees to have them go to the community center's meeting as opposed to coming here. I haven't heard a peep from him since that conversation," Deacon Roosevelt said.

Ryker looked completely deflated. He didn't know where else to go to try to find Lyriq. He was at his wits end. He looked up when he felt the deacon's hand on his shoulder.

"Go home, son, and trust that God will bring your bride home to you. While you're there waiting, ask God to strengthen your wife and to increase her level of discernment. Everyone operating in your life shouldn't be allowed to operate on such a high level," the deacon warned rather ominously before walking away.

Ryker watched the deacon ease out of view, but ultimately blew off his warning as the ramblings of an old man. He did, however, take the deacon's advice about going home and waiting. He had to have faith Lyriq would return home safely and this entire afternoon was spent worrying in vain.

CHAPTER 22

One o'clock in the morning found Ryker on the phone with the police, trying to file a missing person's report. To his dismay, they'd refused his request, stating his wife had to be missing for more than twenty-four hours. Unless he could provide some type of unusual or suspicious circumstances, there was nothing they could do. She was, after all, a grown woman who had the right to decide how long she wanted to be gone from home, or if she wanted to return at all. The officer on the phone suggested he try and track her with the "Share My Location" feature on his cell phone but had nothing else to offer after Ryker advised she'd obviously turned the feature off.

Ryker sat on the floor full of emotions that he couldn't seem to control. He wanted to punch the walls, he wanted to cry, he wanted to plead to God to bring his wife home. He sat with his head in his hands, wondering if his wife was dead in some gutter. When he couldn't shake the worst-case scenarios from his head, he reached for his keys, but the ringing of his phone changed the direction of his movement. He snatched up the phone and slid his finger across the screen to answer.

"Hello?"

"Hi son, it's your mom. Is everything okay?"

"Mom, what are you doing calling so late? You all right?"

He Won't Go

"I'm fine, but you're not. The Spirit wouldn't let me sleep, what's going on, son?"

"Mom, everything's okay, there's nothing for you to worry about."

"Why are you lying to me? I know something is wrong. Please just tell me, I may be able to help."

"You can't help, Mom. I fear only God can help," Ryker's voice cracked.

"Is Lyriq using again?"

"I don't know, she left home headed for a late lunch with a friend and hasn't come back. She's turned her phone off and I have no idea where to find her. She did slip a week ago but joined Narcotics Anonymous and attended two meetings this week. I thought we were on the right path, but I don't know anything anymore, Mom."

Constance inhaled and exhaled deeply, and Ryker braced himself for the flood of "I told you so's," he predicted would stream from her mouth. But instead, Constance instructed her son to bow his head and she proceeded to lead them in prayer.

"Father, in the mighty name of Jesus, we come before you to first give thanks for all that you have done for us. You are a good God, a merciful God and we praise you, Lord God. Father, you know all things and can do all things. We come before Your throne asking for the safe return of our Lyriq. She's lost right now, Father, and we

151

ask You to protect her from all hurt, harm, and danger. We ask You, Lord, to lead her back home. Give her the comfort of knowing that she will be met with love and understanding. We know she is ill, and we ask You to be a healer right now, Lord. Touch her, strengthen her, and please lead her home. In the matchless name of Jesus, we pray. Amen."

"Thank you, Mom."

"I'm here for you, Ryker, and I can be there if you need or want me to be. Just say the word and I'll book a flight."

"I appreciate that, but I'd like to give it a little more time. If she were to discover that family was in town, it might keep her away as opposed to making her feel safe to return. But please do me one favor, Mom?"

"Of course, what do you need?"

"Just keep praying."

"I will, son. I promise I will. Please let me know when she returns home. I love you," Constance said softly before disconnecting the call.

Ryker stood, placed the phone in his pocket, and grabbed his keys. He couldn't just continue to sit there; he had to try and find her, even if it meant driving aimlessly around the city. He pulled the front door open and was shocked when Lyriq's limp body fell across the threshold. Someone had obviously left her propped up against the door, but how had he not heard them? How long had she been sitting there? Ryker knelt down and gathered his disheveled wife up into his arms. He kicked the door closed and carried her to the sofa.

"Lyriq, come on, baby, wake up. Wake up, Lyriq," he said as he gently patted her face. When she didn't respond, his pat became more of a smack, hoping it would jolt her awake. He ran and got a cold towel, but even that wasn't enough to rouse her. Not knowing what else to do, he dialed 911. Within ten minutes, the police and paramedics were there, checking her vitals and questioning Ryker about what happened.

"I literally opened the door and she fell through the doorway. I was on my way back out to look for her, but there she was slumped against the door. She has a history of drug use," he advised. "I don't know what else could be wrong. Please help her," he begged.

"We'll do all we can, sir. We're going to transport her to the medical center, you can follow us there," one of the paramedics advised.

"Not so fast," an officer said. "We have a few questions."

"Well, you'll have to meet me at the medical center, because I'm following them right now," Ryker said bluntly as he followed the stretcher into the hall, locking the door behind him.

Thirty minutes later, the officers approached Ryker as he sat in the emergency waiting room, filling out insurance and medical history documents.

Stacey Covington-Lee

"We know this is a difficult time for you, Mr. Adams, but do you mind if we ask you a few questions?" The big-bellied officer asked.

"I'll tell you what I can, but I honestly don't know much," Ryker responded with annoyance in his voice and plastered across his face.

"Do you know who could've dropped your wife at the door, or why they would just leave her like that?"

"Like I said, I don't know much. What I do know is that she went out to lunch with her friend, Bailey. That's the same woman who later answered my wife's phone and told me she was unavailable. As for who brought my wife home, I have no clue, but it's safe to assume her friend isn't strong enough to carry her through the doors, to the elevator, and to our door. Maybe if you all had taken my missing person call seriously, she wouldn't be in this condition now," Ryker barked.

"Sir, I'm sure they told you, your wife is an adult and has a right to leave home and stay away as long as she likes. Seems to me your anger is pointed in the wrong direction," the big-bellied officer retorted.

"I understand that but clearly, she encountered some type of danger, or we wouldn't be here. If someone tells the cops a loved one is in danger, aren't y'all supposed to do something?" When there was no reply, Ryker continued with a harsh toned, "I thought so."

He Won't Go

Just as Ryker returned his attention to the paperwork, one of the emergency room physicians approached and called his name. Ryker jumped to his feet, anxious to hear what the doctor had to say. "Is she going to be all right?" He asked.

The doctor extended his hand and introduced himself as Ryker returned his greeting with a firm handshake. "So, how is my wife, will she be okay?" Ryker asked again.

"Mr. Adams it appears that your wife has been drugged. She has extremely high levels of gamma hydroxybutyric acid, also known as GHB, in her system. So much so, it has slowed her heart rate as well as her breathing. Because of the amount in her system, we're currently administering physostigmine, which is a reversal drug. It should aid in getting the GHB out of her system."

Ryker was rubbing his head as if he were having trouble computing what the doctor was saying. "Doctor, correct me if I'm wrong, but isn't GHB the date rape drug?"

The doctor dropped his eyes before looking back up at Ryker. "Yes sir, it is. Once we've successfully reversed some of the effects of the drug and stabilized her breathing and heart rate, one of our specialized nurses will administer an exam to determine if your wife has been sexually assaulted." The doctor gave Ryker a consoling pat on his shoulder. "We'll be sure to update you as soon as we can on her condition." He removed his hand from Ryker's shoulder and walked away.

Ryker stumbled back to the chair and plopped down with his elbows on his knees and his head in his hands. He was trying to fight the tears that were threatening to spill from his eyes. Of all the things he feared when he couldn't find Lyriq, this had never entered his mind. Who did this to his wife and where in the world was Bailey when all of this was happening? What hand did she play in this assault?

"I'm very sorry about all of this, Mr. Adams, and I promise we'll do all we can to find the responsible party," the big-bellied officer assured, even though he knew Ryker had no faith in his words.

Ryker provided what little information he could to the officer and watched as the guy and his little note pad waddled out the emergency room doors. Another two agonizing hours passed before the doctor reemerged with an update on Lyriq. He advised Ryker that they were able to reverse some of the effects of the GHB, and Lyriq was in stable condition.

"Were you all able to determine if she was raped?" Ryker asked, not daring to breathe until he heard the doctor's reply.

"We were able to determine that Mrs. Adams has had sex within the last twenty-four to forty-eight hours, but there was no apparent trauma that would indicate she'd been raped. We expect her to make a full recovery but would like to keep her for observation for a day or two."

He Won't Go

A sense of relief washed over Ryker's face. "When will I be able to see her?" He quizzed.

"Follow me, I'll take you to her. However, I will ask that you keep the visit short. She needs her rest and no offense, but it looks like you could use a little sleep yourself."

"I can't argue with that," Ryker grunted as he stopped in front of the hospital room door the doctor had directed him to.

"Remember, keep it short. You can come back for a longer visit later in the day," the doctor instructed.

"Yes, Doctor, and thank you so much for everything."

Ryker stepped into Lyriq's room and gave a silent prayer of thanks. She looked weak and tired. Her eyes fluttered open and filled with tears when he came into focus. He kissed her forehead and whispered, "Everything's going to be okay." He hoped his words sounded believable and comforting to his wife because they certainly felt empty to him.

CHAPTER 23

Ryker returned to his condo and as he stepped to the door, he spotted a phone. Assuming it was Lyriq's, he snatched it up. He watched curiously as a sticky note fell off the back of the phone and drifted to the floor. He picked it up and read the scribble. *If you want to keep your wife alive and well, tell her to stay away from Bailey.* Ryker balled the note up and pounded his fist on the door. He was furious that Lyriq deliberately lied to him about staying away from the drama. He was pissed that she'd put herself in harm's way and was so reckless with her recovery.

He let himself into the condo and chucked the note in the trash. He went to put the phone down, but the illuminating screen piqued his interest. Was someone texting her? He punched in her code and read, *Please let me know that you're okay. I'm really sorry about everything. Please call me.* The message was from Bailey, and it took everything in his power to not throw the phone and smash it against the wall. He inhaled deeply and slowly released his breath. Instead of destroying the phone, he decided to use it to call Bailey.

"Hello, Lyriq, are you okay?"

"Bailey, how is it that you sound just fine, but my wife is in the hospital recovering from an overdose?" Ryker's voice was so calm it was almost scary.

He Won't Go

"I…I'm sorry," Bailey stammered. "I never meant for any of this to happen. I simply wanted to see my baby girl. I never imagined harm would come to anyone, especially Lyriq. Is she going to be okay?"

"Bailey, just tell me who did this to her. How did this come about?"

She took deep breaths to steady herself and to stall as she tried to decide if she wanted to tell Ryker half-truths or be completely honest.

"Bailey!" Ryker barked into the phone.

"I'm sorry," Bailey squealed. Her heart pounded out of fear and guilt. "Lyriq came over to tell me about you all's encounter at dinner Friday night, but Craig was already here. He invited Lyriq to sit down and join us while we discussed the possibility of me seeing my daughter. We were sipping on some Cognac, and he asked Lyriq to join us. When she declined, he told her that if she wanted to help me then she needed to be a little more friendly, a little more social. He went and poured her a drink and must've slipped something in it. The next thing I knew, Lyriq could barely keep her eyes open, couldn't even talk. Every time she seemed to be coming around, he'd force her to drink more." Bailey began to sob. "I begged him to leave her alone and he said he would but only if I cooperated." Her sobs grew deeper, almost uncontrollable. "He raped me over and over again. I didn't fight back, it was the only way to keep him from hurting Lyriq," Bailey sobbed and heaved.

159

"I'm sorry, Bailey. I'm so sorry that happened to you, but Lyriq was still terribly hurt," Ryker said in a softer tone.

"I tried to protect her, I promise. I thought she'd just sleep off whatever it was that he gave her. I thought the drug would be better than the physical abuse. I'm sorry. I'm so sorry," she moaned as her body shook with tears."

"You need to report him, Bailey. I'll come get you and take you to the police station. I'll stay with you while they take your statement," Ryker offered.

"I can't, he agreed to let me see my little girl. If I report him, not only will he keep my daughter from me, but I'll be lucky if he doesn't kill me. He's not to be played with or threatened. He has goons everywhere, no one will be able to protect me, not even the cops. Reporting him isn't an option and it shouldn't be for Lyriq either."

"You do what you feel you need to do, Bailey, and I'll do what I need to do for the safety and protection of my wife."

"Ryker, he knows where she lives. If you report him, it'll be like putting a gun to Lyriq's head. I'm begging you to leave it alone. Be thankful she wasn't hurt any more than she was and leave it alone," Bailey warned before disconnecting the call.

In frustration and anger, Ryker threw the phone and after crashing into the wall, it fell in pieces to the floor. He fell to the sofa and dropped his head into his hands. He didn't know how he could walk away from this. He didn't know how he could let this goon go unchecked, unpunished for what he'd done to Lyriq. Ryker had felt hurt before, dealt with immeasurable pain, but never the level of anger he was feeling now. It was all consuming and directed at so many people, but none more than the animal that had hurt his wife. As he contemplated what he should do next, there was a knock at the door. He bounced over and snatched the door open, only to find the rotund cop standing on the other side.

"Hello, Mr. Adams, I thought I'd stop by on my way to the station to see if you'd learned any more about who may have drugged your wife. Have you received any messages, threats, or related information of any kind?"

Ryker pondered the question and then replayed his conversation with Bailey over in his head. His sights turned to the crumpled note in the waste basket and broken phone on the floor.

"Mr. Adams?" The officer called out, yanking Ryker from his thoughts.

"Um, no, I haven't heard or learned anything new. But I have your card and will call you if I learn anything more about the situation."

"Please do, Mr. Adams, and as soon as she's up to it, I'll need to interview your wife."

"I understand." Ryker acknowledged, but all he could think about was how he needed to have a conversation with Lyriq before the cops did.

"What happened to the phone?" The round cop asked as he nodded towards the broken pieces on the floor.

"What can I say, frustration got the better of me," Ryker confessed.

"I can understand that. Well, here's another card, call me if you learn of anything new and definitely call when your wife is ready for a conversation." The cop turned towards the door and tipped his tacky summer hat to Ryker as he existed the condo.

Unable to think clearly, Ryker huffed through the bedroom and into the bath where he turned on the shower and stripped before stepping underneath the waterfall. He'd hoped the beads of water would pound the stress from his body and help ease his mind, but that was a little too much to hope for. All it did was clean his body. He dried off, pulled on some lounge pants, and fell onto the bed. Exhausted, he dozed off and managed to sleep for a whopping two hours before his eyes fluttered open.

CHAPTER 24

Lying on the bed staring at the ceiling, Ryker prayed for sleep to overtake him again. But sleep wouldn't come. His mind kept replaying Bailey's recap of events. Had she really put herself in harm's way to protect Lyriq? Why had Lyriq defied his wishes, why had she lied to him? How would he ever be able to trust anything that comes out of her mouth again? How was he supposed to let this all go and not tell the cops all he knew? Why hadn't he turned over the crumpled note as proof of that animal's threats? The questions just kept coming and Ryker's spirit became increasingly unsettled.

It was well past noon. He had missed church but needed to hear a word from The Lord more than ever. Ryker picked up his Bible but didn't open it. He held it to his chest as if the words would seep through the cover and into his soul, and renew his spirit. He held the Word of God and asked for strength, for clarity, for guidance. He cried and he prayed. Eventually, he placed the Bible back on the nightstand and picked up his phone. After Pastor Carlton agreed to meet him at the hospital, Ryker dressed, gulped down a bitter cup of coffee, and left.

Lyriq was sitting up in bed when Ryker arrived, looking considerably better than she had when he'd left her earlier. He walked to her bedside, bent down, and planted a sweet kiss on her forehead. His anger, frustration, and doubt, while still burning inside, subsided considerably when she smiled at him meekly.

"Baby, I need you to tell me what happened yesterday," Ryker said more demanding than questioning. I need to hear from your beautiful lips what happened."

Immediately, Lyriq's eyes welled with tears. He grabbed a tissue and lovingly dabbed her face dry, but he didn't let her off the hook. He lowered himself onto the side of her bed and urged her along. "Tell me, Lyriq, tell me exactly what happened."

Lyriq adjusted herself in bed and looked directly into Ryker's eyes. "I went over to Bailey's to share the events of Friday night. I didn't know she had company. I never expected to find her baby's father there, especially after all the horrible things she'd said about him." Lyriq choked back tears. "I'm so sorry I lied to you. I'm sorry I went over there; my intention was to help. I'm so sorry."

"Baby, just tell me what happened," Ryker urged.

"When I saw she wasn't alone, I tried to leave. I told her I'd call her later, but that Craig guy told me to come in. He said if I wanted things to work out for Bailey, I'd come in and join them for a drink. Babe, it's not like he was taking no for an answer. He poured drinks and I remember so little after that. I have flashes of him on top of Bailey, of her crying, of him pouring something in my mouth, and of being picked up by…you," she said with furrowed brows as Pastor Carlton stepped to the entrance of her room.

He Won't Go

Ryker's eyes followed the direction of Lyriq's, and he thought that she was surely confused. "No baby, he's here to pray with us."

"But he picked me up from the floor and said something about it being ok, didn't you, Pastor? Weren't you there, didn't you save me?"

Ryker stood to his feet and looked at Pastor Carlton with a mix of confusion and anger etched across his face. He inhaled deeply, blew out a slow, steady breath before asking Pastor Carlton exactly what was going on.

"Good afternoon good people. Lyriq, I'm glad to see you looking so well. Your husband here had me scared, had me concerned you were far worse than you appear to be now," Pastor Carlton chuckled nervously.

"Please understand that I am not in the mood for pleasantries, Pastor. I am, however, in desperate need of answers. Were you with Lyriq, Bailey, and this Craig character yesterday and if so, why?"

"Ryker, when you came to the church, I was very upfront with you about my past, my addictions, the bad company I used to keep. Well, Craig Garrison was part of that past."

"You keep saying past, Pastor, and I'm talking about the here and now. What the hell is going on now? Did you see my wife yesterday? Did you participate in drugging her? Are you still using and, or selling drugs? Are you to blame for Lyriq's condition?"

Lyriq sat up even straighter in bed. "Ryker, I didn't see Pastor Carlton when I arrived at Bailey's yesterday. He wasn't there…" She dropped her head and rubbed her eyes trying to remember. "…not at first. I…I must be confused, babe."

"Lyriq, just relax. Pastor Carlton is about to clear all of this up right now, aren't you, Pastor?" The look on Ryker's face and tense stance of his body let Pastor Carlton know even though phrased as a question, Ryker was demanding answers.

"Please sit," Pastor Carlton motioned towards the bed as he pulled up a chair for himself. He sat, crossed his legs, and took a deep breathe. "I was there yesterday. I honestly have no idea how long you'd been at Bailey's before Craig called me and asked me to come over and help him out. When I arrived, you were slumped over on the floor," he explained as he looked sorrowfully at Lyriq. "I asked him what was going on, but all he would say is you were meddling in business that wasn't yours. He told me to get you out of there before something bad happened to you."

"Something bad did happen to her," Ryker barked.

"It could've been much worse," Pastor Carlton replied with an expression that told Ryker to chill out. "Your friend, Bailey, wasn't as lucky. It was clear she'd been horrifically abused in more ways than one. He wouldn't let me near her, he wouldn't let her leave.

He Won't Go

Lyriq, when you started mumbling and seemed to have recognized me, he forced more of whatever he had given you down your throat. I told him it was okay and to just step off. That is when I picked you up and left. I drove around with you for a while. I wanted to take you to the hospital but didn't know what explanation I'd offer up to the staff. I remembered Deacon Roosevelt left me a message that you'd been by, Ryker. He said you were looking for your wife. That's when I decided to prop Lyriq up against your door. It was the safest thing I could think to do without bringing unwanted attention and questions to any of us."

"But why, of all the people in Irvine, would that thug call you?" Ryker asked.

"Just because I'm a changed man doesn't mean I'm not still tied to that world in some ways. For a long time, I worked for Craig. Then I started using the product I was supposed to be selling. That's an offense usually punishable by death out in the streets. But Craig let me live, allowed me to get clean, he even invested in the church so we could initially get the doors open all because his mother, Betty, is my mom's best friend. By investing in the church, by letting me live, it indebted me to him for the rest of my life. I'll never be free of him, at least not until one of us dies." Pastor Carlton dropped his head as if the realization of his statement had just hit him for the first time.

With tears free flowing down her face, Lyriq asked about her friend. "What did he do with Bailey? Is she still alive?"

Ryker pulled her close. "Yes, I've talked to Bailey. That animal hurt her, but she is going to be okay. She even said he's going to let her see her daughter." Ryker kissed Lyriq on the forehead and told her to try and relax.

"Tell me this, Carlton, when I got Lyriq from the hall there was no cell phone. But when I got back from the hospital, her cell phone was there with a note attached. Where did that come from?"

"That sounds like a question I need to know the answer to as well," the big-bellied cop interjected as he waddled into Lyriq's room.

Both Ryker and Pastor Carlton stood to their feet. "Pastor Carlton, this is officer... I'm sorry, what was your name again?" Ryker asked.

"Actually, it's Detective Vasquez," he said with an extended hand.

Pastor Carlton accepted his handshake. "Nice to meet you detective, I was about to tell Ryker that I found the phone outside his building when I went by to check on him. I recognized Lyriq's distinctive case."

Ryker listened in amazement at how easily the lies rolled off Pastor Carlton's tongue. It was like he didn't have a saved bone in his body.

He Won't Go

"I thought I heard you say something about a note," Detective Vasquez nodded towards Ryker. But Pastor Carlton chimed in before Ryker could open his mouth.

"I'd just scribbled a note of encouragement for Ryker here. I wanted him to know I'd been by and that I was praying for Sister Lyriq."

"I see," The detective remarked. "Mrs. Adams, do you feel up to answering a few questions so we can find out who did this to you?"

"I'm so sorry, detective, but I honestly can't remember anything beyond having an afternoon Mimosa with my friend. Next thing I know, I'm waking up in the hospital."

"Do you remember the male that was also at your friend's house?"

"I don't know his name, but I remember him being an average height, slim built young man. I know that's not much of a description, but it's the best I can do," Lyriq sniffled.

Ryker rubbed his head in dismay. What kind of people had he invited into his life? He was again disturbed at how easily the lies fell from the lips around him. He wanted so badly to scream the truth from the top of his lungs, but he stifled himself and let the lies play out in front of him.

"I see. Can you at least give me your friend's full name and address?" Detective Vasquez asked.

Stacey Covington-Lee

"Of course. Her name is Bailey Cooper, and she lives at the corner of Main and Jamboree. Sorry I can't be more specific, but her exact address is in my phone."

"Mr. Adams, any chance you have your wife's phone with you?"

"Remember that phone you saw in pieces, the one I took my frustrations out on? Well, that was her phone. Sorry, but it's in pieces back at the condo."

Again, Detective Vasquez mumbled, "I see," surely his way of communicating that he did not believe anything he'd just heard. "Thanks for the information and just know I'll be following back up with you all real soon." Vasquez tilted his hat and left the room.

Pastor Carlton waited until he was sure the detective was out of ear-shot and whipped out his phone. "The cops know your name and address, you need to leave now!"

"So, you'll lie to the cops, but help your thuggish friends? Are those behaviors they taught you in seminary school?" Ryker quizzed sarcastically.

"That wasn't a thug, that was Bailey, and I was making an effort to protect her."

"Now I'm really confused. The note you left on Lyriq's phone said to stay away from Bailey. If she's such bad news, then why are you trying to protect her?"

He Won't Go

"Ryker, I didn't leave a note. That must have been Craig's handy work. And the only reason I'd ever want Lyriq to stay away from Bailey is because Craig will never leave her alone. That puts anyone connected with Bailey at risk. That's the only reason I would encourage you to stay away, Lyriq. Not because Bailey is some horrible person. To the contrary, she's a smart, beautiful woman whose life was headed for greatness. Then she met Craig and he changed everything for her. He's the horrible one."

Tears once again stung Lyriq's eyes. She knew what a good soul Bailey was, she'd felt it when they first met. It hurt her heart to know that Bailey had sacrificed herself to save her from a worse fate. It hurt even worse to know she couldn't do anything to help save Bailey in return.

CHAPTER 25

After spending the day at the hospital, Ryker was finally dragging himself through the door of the condo. He'd hoped to bring Lyriq home with him, but the doctor wanted to run a few more blood tests before releasing her. He dropped his takeout order on the table and headed for the shower. All he wanted was to bathe, eat, and sleep. Just as he turned on the water and began to disrobe, the doorbell rang. He turned off the water and grumbled all the way to the door, ready to snatch it open and bless out anyone who'd dared to darken it.

"Who is it?" He barked.

"It's me, baby, it's your mama."

Completely unable to hide his annoyance and frustration, Ryker snatched the door open and in a tone much harsher than he intended to use, he asked, "Mama, what are you doing here?"

"Clearly intruding. I'll get a hotel room for the night, and we'll try this again tomorrow." Without waiting for a reply, Constance turned and headed for the elevator.

"Mama no," Ryker pled as he quickly darted and grabbed her by the arm. "I'm sorry, Mama, I was just caught off guard. Please come on back." He grabbed her bags and led her back to his home. "Are you hungry?"

He Won't Go

"No, I grabbed dinner at one of the airport eateries."

"You want to keep me company while I wolf down some take out?" Ryker tried to smile wistfully.

"I think it's been a long day for both of us, son. Why don't you place my bags in the guest room for me? I'll head to bed, and we'll get a fresh start in the morning. How does that sound?"

"Sounds good, Mama." Ryker did as Constance had asked and before leaving her alone in the room, he leaned in and placed a sweet kiss on her cheek. "I love you, Mama."

"I love you too, baby."

CHAPTER 26

Ryker picked Lyriq up from the hospital at noon. She was still a tad weak, but nothing like she was when he'd found her propped against their door. Once he'd gotten her situated in the car, he headed towards home. They rode in silence as he contemplated how to tell her that his mother was at the condo waiting to take care of her. He knew Lyriq would hit the roof, but he also knew his mother's heart was in the right place.

"Babe, I need to say some things, to make you aware of some new developments. This is going to be hard to hear, but I don't want you blindsided."

Before he could finish, Lyriq cut him off. "Oh God, are you divorcing me? Are you about to tell me you're leaving me, Ryker? I know I messed up, but babe, please don't let this end us."

"End us? You are my wife, we took vows. Yes, this is a challenging situation, but nothing is going to end us. We're going to figure out our best course of action and work through this," Ryker assured as he gave her hand a reassuring squeeze.

Lyriq released a sigh of relief. Knowing he was going to be by her side, she'd be able to handle whatever new so-called developments he was referring to. "So, what is it you don't want me to be blindsided by?"

He Won't Go

"We have an unexpected house guest."

Lyriq crumpled her face in confusion, unable to imagine who would be crashing at their place at a time like this. "Who?"

Looking straight ahead, Ryker replied timidly, "My mother."

"Oh God, help me!" Lyriq sank back into her seat and dropped her head in her hands. It was all she could do to keep from screaming. She could only imagine the conversations that had taken place between Ryker and Constance. Surely, she had taken this opportunity to scream "I told you so," at the top of her lungs while trying to persuade Ryker to ship his drug addicted wife back to Georgia on a Greyhound bus. Lyriq's head spun as she wondered how many times Constance had mentioned the word annulment in the course of the last few hours. Had Constance already trashed her name to anyone that would listen back home? Lyriq's eyes welled with tears at the thought of what Constance had told her parents. "I can't do it, Ryker, I can't face your mother. I'm not physically or mentally capable of going to battle with her right now."

"I was concerned too, babe, but she's not here to battle against us, she's here to battle with us. She is concerned for your well-being and wants to help. I know you're skeptical and rightfully so, but trust me, I wouldn't allow her to stay if I wasn't sure her intentions were pure."

"How did she even get here so fast? Did you call her before you even called the police?"

Stacey Covington-Lee

"No, it wasn't like that. You'd been missing for several hours. I'd contacted the police and was about to head out to look for you again when she called me. She called to check in and see how we were doing but knew something was wrong by my voice. I couldn't hide how angry I was, how scared I was. She asked what was wrong, I told her, and she led me in prayer for your safe return. Next thing I know, she's ringing the doorbell." He took her hand and brought it to his lips. With a gentle kiss, he promised Lyriq, "Her intentions are pure."

As they approached the door to their home, Lyriq's left eye began to twitch uncontrollably. She tried placing a finger on it and rubbing gently, but that eye had a mind of its own. Before Ryker could place the key in the lock, the door swung open. Lyriq stood there looking like a deer in headlights but felt a sense of calm rush over her when Constance ushered her in and wrapped her in a motherly embrace.

"I'm so glad you're okay, Lyriq. I'm thankful to God for returning you to us."

Lyriq returned the embrace. "Thank you, Constance, and thank you for your prayers."

Constance ordered Ryker to help Lyriq with a shower and dressing in comfortable lounge wear while she finished preparing a late brunch of biscuits, salmon croquettes, grits, eggs, and coffee. Lyriq emerged from her bedroom feeling more refreshed than she thought possible in her still weakened state. She took a seat at the table and prayed Constance wouldn't be insulted by her inability to consume large portions of food.

"I've got plenty here to help you regain your strength," Constance offered.

"Thank you so much, Constance, but my stomach is still a tad queasy. May I just have a biscuit and a cup of coffee?"

"Of course. We'll ease into the food thing and build your tolerance a little at a time." Just as Constance placed a cup of coffee on the table for Lyriq, Ryker emerged from the bedroom and joined them. "Would you like anything, son?"

"I want everything, Mama," Ryker replied as he rubbed his hands together in anticipation of all the goodness his mother had prepared.

The rest of the day was mostly spent with Ryker and Constance watching Lyriq sleep and Constance pulling the last few details of everything that had happened out of her son. Once he'd spilled all the beans, Constance's only question was, "What do we do now?"

CHAPTER 27

The next morning, as they lay in bed, Ryker tried his best to comfort and reassure Lyriq that everything would be fine while he was away. "I promise not to work a full day, babe, but I've got to go into the office for a little while and I've got to stop by the church to retrieve your keys from Carlton. It's my understanding that he left your car parked in the church lot."

"Don't you mean Pastor Carlton?"

"I mean what I said. Until I can get a better understanding of his involvement with these thugs and why I wasn't made aware of it before investing funds in this church, he's just Carlton. The Pastor part is very much up in the air for me."

Lyriq chose not to explore the conversation further, but inside, her heart was breaking. So much in Ryker's life was being turned upside down all because of her. He loved that church and now even it and its leadership were questionable for him. She was supposed to be his help meet, but it seemed she'd only managed to become a heavy load of stress for her husband.

She watched him dress and as he prepared to walk out the door, she prayed for peace to abide between she and Constance in his absence.

He Won't Go

Thirty minutes after Ryker left, Lyriq decided to stop procrastinating and join Constance at the kitchen table. "Good morning, Constance, how are you today?"

"I'm fine, Lyriq. The question is, how are you? Are you feeling rested, a little stronger than yesterday?"

"Yes ma'am, thankfully, I'm feeling much better."

"I was going to prepare a light breakfast; do you think you'll be able to stomach some food?"

"Now Constance, we both know you don't cook anything light. You go all out for every meal," Lyriq chuckled.

Constance didn't try to stifle her laughter. Lyriq was right and she knew it. "Well to be honest, I was going to make some cheese grits with sausage, toast, and eggs. I squeezed a couple of oranges for fresh juice before you came out."

The ladies laughed hardily as Constance sat a glass of fresh juice in front of her daughter-in-law. She walked back to the counter and began to prepare their food. The two shared small talk for the thirty minutes it took Constance to finish cooking. Once she was done, she placed a heaping plate of food right under Lyriq's nose.

"Mumm, this looks and smells delicious. Thank you."

"You're welcome, now eat up. Lord knows an extra pound or two won't hurt you. Let the food fortify your body and warm your soul."

Stacey Covington-Lee

Lyriq knew she'd dropped a couple of pounds over the course of the past few days and tried not to let the "extra pound or two" comment bother her. But what was bothering her was not knowing what Constance had shared with her parents and community back home. She'd been imagining the worst, but not knowing for sure was driving her crazy. She inhaled deeply and asked, "Constance, would you mind sharing with me exactly what you told my parents about my situation?" She braced herself for Constance's response.

"I haven't talked to your parents, Lyriq. What happened to you, the fall-out from the situation, and whatever will happen next, it's all your story, it's not my story to tell. The only person that even knows I'm here is my best friend, and she thinks I came for an impromptu visit. When I tell you I'm here to help, I mean it. I just want to support you and help however I can," Constance reassured her with a loving pat of her hand.

Lyriq exhaled a breath of relief. "You have no idea how much I appreciate that, Constance. I'd hate for my parents to be back home worried sick about me. And I promise to share this story with them, I just want to get on the other side of it first."

"If you never tell them, that's your business. No one will ever hear about it from me."

CHAPTER 28

The knock on the door snatched Ryker from his thoughts. He looked up to see Kane staring at him curiously. "You all right, bruh?"

"Yeah man, just got a lot on my mind. The weekend was pretty wild and left me with a lot on my plate." Ryker went on to give Kane a brief run-down of the weekend's events. He couldn't help but notice that the more he talked, the more Kane's facial expression changed to that of a deer caught in headlights. He never meant to share so much, but Kane was his best friend and he needed to confide in someone.

"Your plate in indeed full, my man, but I'm here to help. Tell me what I can do? How can I help you through this situation?"

"Kane, I think that only God will get us through this, but I would appreciate a ride over to the church so I can retrieve Lyriq's car."

"Consider it done. I'm ready to leave whenever you are."

"Thanks. I just want to work on a couple things and then we can head out," Ryker said.

"You know, if you need to take some time off, I can hold down the fort," Kane offered.

Stacey Covington-Lee

"I appreciate it, man, but right now work is a welcomed distraction," Ryker confessed.

By noon, Ryker was climbing into the passenger side of his best friend's ride ready to not only pick up Lyriq's car, but to have a serious talk with Carlton. Ryker broke through the background music that played and confided what was upsetting him most was the fact that he couldn't do anything to the trash dealer that drugged Lyriq. To his disappointment, Kane agreed with Pastor Carlton, Lyriq, and Bailey. It was best to let it go, otherwise someone would be made an example of, and he didn't want to see anyone hurt any more than they already had been. When they arrived at the church, Ryker asked Kane if he wanted to come inside with him.

"Nah, bruh, you know church buildings aren't really my thing. Too many devils roaming around inside. Apparently, one of those devils is your pastor, so watch your back."

Ryker wasn't in the mood or the right mind space to debate the church and its place in society with Kane right now, so instead, he told Kane he wouldn't be long and headed towards the church offices. He went through the side door but detoured towards the main sanctuary. Ryker took a seat on the front pew and bowed his head in prayer. He asked God for direction, clarity, and understanding. As he said, "Amen," he felt a presence to the right of him.

"Hey there, young man. I didn't expect to see you here until later this afternoon," Deacon Roosevelt chimed.

He Won't Go

"Hey Deacon, I didn't know you were expecting me at all," Ryker admitted with an expression of surprise contorting his face.

"Pastor Carlton stopped by earlier and wanted me to make sure you got your wife's car keys."

Ryker made no attempt to hide his anger and annoyance. "So, he's not here, he just passed the keys off to you, Deacon? That coward piece of---"

Deacon Roosevelt cleared his throat as a means of preventing Ryker from finishing his statement. "Is it that he's a coward, or is he giving you the space you need to think through the events of the weekend and time to try and understand the position he's in?"

"So, you're aware of the fact that he's involved with a known drug dealer and the same dealer caused serious physical harm to my wife and her friend this weekend?" Ryker barked more than asked.

"Yes, I'm aware. Everyone needs a confidant and I'm Pastor Carlton's. I'm probably the only person he fully trusts because I see him for what he is, Ryker. I first see him for the imperfect man he is and then I see him for the minister that he is. The minister that's chasing God's heart and trying to make a difference the best way he knows how, despite the difficult position he's been put in."

"But Deacon Roosevelt, he used drug money to establish this church. He allowed me to invest in this church without fully disclosing his past and how he is still, and likely always will be, attached to someone as evil as this drug dealing thug. I don't think all the time in the world will help me to see past that."

"You're right," Deacon Roosevelt confessed. "Pastor Carlton took drug money to establish this church. He took drug money to help establish a drug program that has helped countless people in the community to get clean and back on their feet. He used drug money to open a food pantry and provide for those dealing with food insecurity. He used drug money to establish just about all the programs that helped countless people in this community. Now, it's the tithes and the offerings of the parishioners that keep those programs going. Any drug money that finds its way in here now is put in an account and only used to help the members that fall on hard times and need help paying their rent or utilities."

Deacon Roosevelt waited for Ryker's rebuttal. When there was none, he continued. "Pastor Carlton never solicited the drug money, it was forced on him. So, tell me, Brother Ryker. Would you rather that drug money be used to supply more poison to our community, or used for the up building of God's kingdom? I understand it's a lot to take in and very much unacceptable to some. These are the things that Pastor Carlton want to give you time and space to think about." Deacon Roosevelt placed the keys in Ryker's hand, gave him a fatherly pat on the shoulder, stood and walked away.

Ryker jumped in Lyriq's car and pulled around to where Kane was patiently waiting. He tapped the horn and signaled for Kane to follow him. Shortly afterwards, Ryker parked the car in their garage and jumped back into Kane's car.

"Man, I don't mind waiting while you go up and check on Lyriq and your mom. You might want to make sure they're not ripping each other's hair out," Kane chuckled.

"Right now, I don't care what they do to one another. I need a little more time to think before I head back into that lioness den."

"I take it your talk with the good pastor wasn't as helpful as you'd hoped it would be," Kane quizzed.

Ryker exhaled deeply. "I didn't get to talk to him. He'd left the keys with one of the deacons." Ryker went on to tell Kane all the deacon had shared with him. "I prayed for clarity, but that conversation just left me more confused. At the end of the day, the church was still built with ill-gotten gains, but the things Carlton has done for the community have been phenomenal." Ryker rubbed his head as if that would help clear the cluttered thoughts. "Honestly, I don't even understand why your brother would bother donating to a church in the first place."

If looks could kill, Ryker would've fallen over dead. "He is not my brother," Kane barked with more anger than he intended. "Look man, he is my father's son, but I will never claim that low-life criminal as my brother. I've never had anything to do with him and can't imagine I ever will. As for why he gives to the church, trust me, he's getting something out of it. The good pastor will be able to tell you what that something is."

"My bad, man. I didn't mean to hit a nerve. I know y'all aren't down like that and didn't mean to insinuate you were," Ryker said earnestly.

"No problem, I didn't mean to pop off, man. We're all good."

Ryker worked for another hour or so before deciding to head home. He hoped he wouldn't return to an upset wife and a mother screeching, "I told you so." With so much on his mind, he wanted to walk into a peaceful home. He also wanted Lyriq to be receptive to the information he'd been researching for the past hour, but something told him that she'd take one look, hear one word, and shut him down.

Laughter and lighthearted conversation greeted Ryker as he stepped into the condo. He was both surprised and thankful. He knew his mother better than anyone and he'd assumed by now, her lecturing would've driven Lyriq over the edge. He'd never been so happy to be wrong. Seeing the two of them on the couch chatting it up like old friends made his heart smile. "Want to let me in on the joke?" He teased as he closed the door.

"Hey son, home from work already?" Constance smiled.

Lyriq jumped to her feet and flung her arms around his neck. "Hey babe, how was work? Are you hungry?"

He Won't Go

Ryker held her lovingly. "Work was fine and yes, I am hungry. I haven't had a bite today." He released Lyriq and went to his mom, placing a sweet kiss on her cheek. "Hey, Mama."

"Hey, hon. Constance replied as she rose to her feet. "Here, sit with your wife while I start dinner."

"Let me help you, Constance," Lyriq offered as she started to move in the direction of the kitchen.

Ryker grabbed Lyriq by the hand just as Constance was telling her. "Relax. I've got dinner."

Lyriq plopped down on the couch beside her husband. She kissed him gently before asking if he'd had a productive day. He shrugged and she dropped her head. She knew she'd interrupted every facet of his life, including his work and she felt awful for it. She knew how important his work was to him and she hated how she was distracting him from it.

Sensing the shift in her mood, Ryker made an effort to reassure her his lack of productivity wasn't her fault. "I spent a good part of the morning catching up with Kane, discussing a potential new client. We even stepped out for a bit around noon. Oh yeah, I swung by and picked up your car," he said casually as if it wasn't an interruption to his day. He placed the keys in her hand and continued with their conversation. "We're going to try and hook this prospect in for a meeting by the end of the week."

"Thanks, babe," she replied softly as she balled the keys into her fist. "That'll be great if you can persuade that client to come on board with you and Kane." She turned her attention away from Ryker. "Constance, are you sure I can't help with dinner?"

"I'm sure," Constance called from the kitchen.

Since Lyriq was already in her feelings, Ryker figured he'd may as well bring up the dreadful but necessary conversation about what he'd spent the previous hour researching. He reached down in his briefcase and pulled out what he'd printed from the rehabilitation center's website.

"I wanted to talk to you about something, about how we move on from here. I think it's important we address the fact that, even though involuntarily, you used drugs again. We both know that the re-introduction of drugs into the system can be a slippery slope. But if we act proactively, we can stop this from becoming a bigger issue. So, I did a little research at work," he continued as he showed her the information about the rehab center. "This place is supposed to be the best in the area and---"

Lyriq cut him off mid-sentence. "You want me to go to rehab? Are you serious? I got drugged, almost killed, and now you want to punish me for it? You want to punish the victim?" Her venomous tone was laced with deep strands of hurt.

"Baby, I'm not trying to punish you, I want to help you, I want to help us."

He Won't Go

"That's not what it feels like, Ryker. It feels like you think I did all of this on purpose just for a high. Well, I didn't! This was done to me, I'm the victim here, not some crackhead that went looking for drugs." Lyriq cried as she stood to her feet. She turned around only to see Constance looking down and shaking her head. Seeing her mother-in-law made her feel even worse. Lyriq covered her face and ran off to their bedroom.

Constance went to her bedroom and grabbed her purse. She walked back out and headed for the front door. She paused when she got within a couple of feet of Ryker. "Why would you bring that conversation up in my presence? Do you know how humiliating that must've been for her? You should've either asked me for privacy or taken her to another room," Constance explained before continuing her path to the door.

"Where are you going, Mama?"

"I saw a little café on the corner. I'm going there and pick up some dessert while you talk to your wife in private. I'll be back in an hour or so." Constance didn't wait to hear any rebuttal from Ryker. When the door closed behind her, Ryker sighed deeply and rubbed his temples again, still hoping that would somehow help the situation.

When Constance arrived at the café, she took a seat at the little corner table by the window. It wasn't long before a robust woman, smiling brightly approached the table.

"Good afternoon, ma'am. Can I get you something to drink other than water?"

"Yes, may I please have a cup of coffee?"

"Is that hot or iced coffee?" the waitress asked.

"Oh no, just plain, hot, black coffee for me. None of that fancy or iced stuff," Constance replied.

The waitress smiled her understanding. "I'll be right back with that coffee, ma'am." She tuned and padded off to the retrieve the order. She was back at the table in less than five minutes. "Is there anything else I can get for you, ma'am?"

"I think I'm good for now," Constance assured.

"All right, if you need anything else, my name is Betty and I'll be happy to get it for you."

"Thank you," Constance said with a smile.

Back at the condo, Ryker had crawled up on the bed behind Lyriq and wrapped his arm around her waist. He cuddled her, trying to comfort her and reassure her that he never intended to blame her for what happened. In that moment, he wouldn't vocalize that if she'd only stayed out of Bailey's drama like he'd asked, like she'd promised, none of this would've happened. Instead, he tried to explain that all he wanted was for them to get back on track, for her to be healthy and not tempted by the idea of feeling the high that almost took her out. He apologized sincerely for broaching the subject in front of his mother. He'd never meant to embarrass or belittle her. He didn't tell her he'd secretly hoped his mother would jump in and side with him. He'd thought she would try to persuade Lyriq that rehab was a great idea. He couldn't have been more wrong.

Listening to him apologize and the level of sincerity in his voice prompted Lyriq to turn over and face her husband. As if reading his mind, she apologized. "Ryker, I'm sorry, I know if I'd done as I promised, none of this would've happened. All I wanted to do was help a friend. In my wildest dreams, I didn't imagine things playing out the way they did. But please hear me when I say that rehab is not the answer for me right now. I talked to my principal today and they've given me the rest of the week off to recoup. I want to spend this week with you and your mom, continue to regain my strength, and be ready for work next week. Getting back to my kids, that will be the best therapy for me."

Ryker rubbed her back and pecked her lips. He wanted so badly to believe what he was hearing. He wanted to trust that there would be no desire to experience another high, but his heart knew better. And as hard as he tried, his face couldn't hide the doubt his heart felt.

"Babe, I'm telling you, this is what's best for me. But I know you need to feel comfortable with the situation as well, so how about we compromise? Let's set up a meeting with Pastor Carlton. We'll sort all of this out, try to understand his position and get me back into the NA meetings. I'll double the number of meetings I attend on a weekly basis if that will make you feel more comfortable with it. What do you say?" Lyriq asked, with hope dripping from her words.

Reluctantly, Ryker partially conceded. "We'll set up a meeting with Carlton for Wednesday and see where we are after that, okay?"

"Okay, babe. Thank you and I promise, this is what's best and you'll come to see this time, I'm right. I'm going to immerse myself in The Word and my meetings. That, along with your support, is what will get us back on track," Lyriq assured as she kissed him gently.

Back at the café, Constance finished her second cup of coffee and asked the waitress, Betty, about their pie selection. Of the apple, cherry, and banana cream pies, she learned the strawberry cheesecake was actually their best seller. She asked for a whole cheesecake to go, paid her tab, and took the short walk back to the condo.

CHAPTER 29

The fact that Constance had continued with her supportive, non-judgmental role had meant the world to Lyriq. The pair had shared thought provoking conversations, a few emotional lows when they discussed addiction and how it had so harshly affected their lives. Constance opened up about losing her husband and how it had devasted both she and Ryker. Listening to Constance gave Lyriq a better prospective of how Ryker must be feeling, the fear he must have when it came to her and her addiction. Lyriq confided she was fearful of having to leave their church because of the secrets Pastor Carlton kept and the association he still maintained. Lyriq knew of the love Ryker had for his church family and the bond he developed with Pastor Carlton. The idea of him losing all of that because of her was unbearable.

"Constance, we've got this meeting with Pastor Carlton in a few hours. Will you please come with us?"

"Oh, Lyriq, I don't think I should be there. This is between you, your husband, your pastor, and God."

Ryker stepped from the bedroom and chimed in as he continued to button his sleeve. "We'd both really like for you to accompany us. I could use your support and advise on this one, Mama. Please?"

"Okay, if y'all are sure this is what you want, I'll go."

Stacey Covington-Lee

"Thank you, Constance," Lyriq said as she embraced her mother-in-law.

Ryker finished getting ready for the day and promised the ladies he'd be back by one o'clock to pick them up for their meeting. He left out and hoped that this time, his mother would see his side and chime in on his behalf. He knew Constance didn't play with church and didn't suffer any jackleg preachers. She'd never be able to get comfortable with a minister accepting drug money, straddling the fence between serving God and serving man.

Later that afternoon, as the three parked in the church lot, they observed Pastor Carlton in a heated discussion with some other man. When the other man turned around, it was Craig, the monster that had drugged Lyriq, the man Kane wouldn't claim as family. Ryker immediately became infuriated. His anger was all-consuming, he had to confront this animal. He opened the door and moved to get out of the car when Lyriq grabbed his arm.

"Ryker, no! Let's sit here until he leaves. You can't say anything to him, there's no telling what he'll do to you. Baby, please, you know he has a gun," Lyriq cried.

"Who is that?" Constance asked.

"That's the guy that drugged Lyriq and there's no way I'm letting him leave like nothing is wrong."

Their voices carried from the car and caught the attention of Pastor Carlton and Craig. They both turned to see who the voices in

194

the distance belonged to. When Craig made a step towards their car, Pastor Carlton stepped in his way. The two exchanged angry words and Craig raised his hands to push Pastor Carlton away from him. To everyone's surprise, even Craig's, Pastor Carlton forcefully pushed him back and pointed for him to get in his car and leave. All they could hear clearly was Pastor Carlton shouting, "Leave now!" Craig pointed at Pastor Carlton and said something menacing before turning towards his car. Just before opening his car door, he looked towards Ryker and Lyriq and pointed as if warning them of some pending doom.

It wasn't until after Craig had driven off and was no longer in view, that Lyriq let go of Ryker. She dried her eyes as she told Ryker to calm down and collect himself. He looked back to see Pastor Carlton wipe what must've been beads of sweat and fear from his forehead. Constance looked around in wonderment at the big, beautiful worship center and the apparent foolishness happening in this supposed house of The Lord. Then she thought about the church back home and the foolishness that happens under that roof as well. She said a quick prayer for God to make her understand all the moving parts of this mess and give her clarity so she could properly advise her family.

By the time they made it to the doors of the church, Deacon Roosevelt was standing there, waiting to greet them. He tried to be the calm in the midst of a lot of high emotions. He spoke softly, smiled, and embraced each of them. "Pastor Carlton stepped to the back for a moment, but if you'll come with me, I'll show you to the conference room where we'll meet." He gestured for everyone to enter and take a seat. He then asked the church secretary to retrieve bottles of water for everyone. By the time she brought in the cold water, Pastor Carlton was entering the room. He smiled warmly and took a seat at the head of the conference table. As quickly as he sat, he jumped back up and went to introduce himself to Constance. After the pleasantries, he returned to his seat, sighed, and began to talk.

"Please let me start by apologizing. I am sorry you all had to witness that tense moment with that particular person. I was not aware he would be stopping by. He knows that his presence here is not a welcomed one, but that isn't something I can always control. I also want to thank you for your willingness to come talk. It's my sincere hope that we'll be able to come to a mutual agreement with how we proceed in love, worship, and mutual respect."

"Thank you for meeting with us, Pastor Carlton. This is clearly a difficult situation for all of us. One none of us ever expected to be in," Lyriq replied.

"Why didn't you tell me there was so much drug money floating through this church and why did you ask me to be an investor if Mr. Pusher Man had you covered?" Ryker quizzed in a none-to-friendly tone.

"As I'd previously explained, I didn't really have a choice in the matter. The only reason I'm alive today is by God's grace, and the

He Won't Go

fact that my mother pled for my life to Craig's mother. In the streets, that extension of grace leaves me indebted to him," Pastor Carlton explained. "As for why I accepted your financial assistance with the church, well that's easy. The more money flowing through here that isn't connected to him, the better our chances of eventually pushing him out altogether."

"I understand what you're saying about these streets, that's survival. But that still doesn't explain why you took and are still taking his dirty money. I don't believe your survival was dependent on accepting his money and if it was, make me understand how?"

Pastor Carlton stood from his chair, slowly and methodically moved around the room until he reached the bookshelves. He cleared his throat and asked, "Ryker, have you ever heard anyone speaking about taking back what the devil stole from them?"

"Yes, everyone has. There have been songs made about it," Ryker replied.

"That drug dealing Craig thought that by providing money to this church, it would prevent me from ever going to the cops with information about him. To a degree he was right, I don't want any unnecessary trouble. But for me, taking the money was a way of taking back what the devil has been stealing from this community for years. That old devil has stolen lives from this community. He has stolen hope and peace from this community, by way of that poison Craig and his goons sell. By accepting his dirty money and using it to save some of those stolen lives, restore folks hope, faith, and

197

peace through the programs we've created, we're taking back what has been stolen." Pastor Carlton pulled a Bible from the shelf and flipped through the pages. "Matthew the eleventh chapter, twelfth verse says, 'And from the days of John the Baptist until now the kingdom of heaven suffers violence, and the violent take it by force.' Many believe that to mean that entering God's Kingdom takes strength, courage, unshakable faith, and endurance because of the continuous opposition leveled against God's people. Do you understand we are a part of God's Kingdom; we are His people, and we are constantly under attack? Now, we can either stand here and just guard the gate, hoping for the best or, we as His people can take back what's been stolen. Using what he took from the people of this community for good, is taking back what was stolen," Pastor Carlton declared in a voice so full of emotion, one that begged for Ryker's understanding.

With one hand, Lyriq reached for Ryker and with the other dabbed at tears spilling over from the corners of her eyes. She hoped he'd received Pastor Carlton's explanation with the same open heart she had. Ryker caressed Lyriq's hand but looked to his mother to gauge how she'd received the words spoken by the pastor. He was surprised to see her nodding her head and slightly rocking as if she were in the church pews listening to Sunday morning service.

"I guess I never thought of it in those terms," Ryker confessed. "I just assumed when you left the drugs in the past, you would've left all of the people affiliated with them in the past as well."

He Won't Go

"Brother Ryker, I was always honest about who and what I was and am. Yes, I turned a page in life and started living for The Lord, but I am still a very imperfect man comprised of all my life experiences, the good, bad, and really ugly. That past experience, along with God's word and direction, helps to guide me today. It will always be a part of me. I hope you'll be able to accept that," Pastor Carlton said.

"We are all imperfect people," Constance interjected. "Acceptance is the gift we give to those striving to be their best selves."

Ryker stood and walked over to Pastor Carlton, extending his hand. When the pastor accepted his handshake, Ryker pulled him in for a brotherly hug. "Thank you for this, Pastor Carlton, it's the conversation I desperately needed."

Relief washed over Lyriq. "Now that we have reached this understanding, Pastor Carlton, I'd like to start back with the NA meetings. I need to attend four meetings a week to ensure my sobriety in the face of all that has happened. Will that be possible?"

"Absolutely not. The schedule hasn't changed, we offer two meetings a week, and honestly, that's all you need. While I understand this last encounter with drugs wasn't necessarily of your free will, I think it's a good idea to commit to participating in the program those two days, no exceptions."

"Wait, what do you mean by *wasn't necessarily of my free will*?" I didn't ask for that, none of it," Lyriq declared.

"But you put yourself in a position for it to happen," Pastor Carlton said unapologetically. "We both know we have to be careful of the company we keep, places we go, and situations we allow ourselves to be put in. I know your intention was to help Bailey, but for your own good, her associations make you all's friendship impossible."

Tears ran down Lyriq's cheeks. She hated the thought of turning her back on the only friend she'd made since arriving in California. Ryker could feel her hurt and pulled her into his chest, embracing her in hopes of absorbing some of her pain.

CHAPTER 30

Lyriq's return to work was the best thing she could've done for herself. The kids greeted her with hugs, plenty of questions, and tattletale comments about the substitute and fellow classmates. She assured them she wouldn't be out again anytime soon and that they were starting anew, so there was no need to tell on anyone or report any questionable behavior. Not only were the kids glad to have her back at school, but so were a couple of the other teachers she had started chatting and laughing with before her unexpected departure. At the end of her first week, Carolyn Clay, one of the younger teachers, asked her to meet for lunch over the weekend. Lyriq gladly accepted, thinking this was the perfect opportunity to make a new friend.

Riding home, Lyriq passed the park and saw big dude's car out front. He was standing over some poor soul who was shaking and seemingly begging for whatever strand of poison big dude was offering that day. She was glad she had the strength to drive on by without giving him a second thought. She arrived at the condo to find Constance in her bedroom, packing her bags.

"What are you doing?"

"What does it look like I'm doing?" Constance replied with a giggle.

"It looks like you're packing to leave, but since you haven't discussed that with us, I know that can't be the case," Lyriq snipped back.

"Girl, you act like you're mad at the thought of me leaving," Constance said.

"I'm not mad, but I would like to know what brought this on. You hadn't said anything about leaving today, tomorrow, or even next week for that matter." The level of unhappiness Lyriq felt stunned her. After their rocky start, she'd never expected to feel this connected to her mother-in-law.

Constance smiled and placed the blouse she was folding in her suitcase. She pushed her bags to the side and motioned for Lyriq to sit beside her on the bed. She chuckled at how Lyriq darn near sat in her lap. "You know I can't stay here forever. I came in a time of crisis to be of help and comfort. I hope I was able to achieve that."

"You've been a great help and source of strength. I don't think Ryker and me could've gotten through this without you," Lyriq assured with a squeeze of her hand.

"Then my work is done, and you and your husband need to get back to life as usual. You've completed your first full week back at work, attended two meetings, and you look like the pillar of strength. Not to mention the fact that I've got a life of my own to get back to. God only knows the level of dust that has accumulated in that house and the juicy gossip I've missed at church," Constance chuckled.

He Won't Go

"Have you told Ryker you're leaving? Did he purchase your plane ticket?"

"No, I just decided last night that it was time to go back home, so I got online and purchased my own non-refundable ticket for Sunday. That way y'all couldn't talk me out of leaving. I want to go to church with you two on Sunday and then you can drop me off at the airport for my five o'clock flight home."

"While I wish you would stay a little while longer, I understand you want to get back. There is nothing like being in your own home with all of your own things," Lyriq acknowledged. "But if you're not leaving until Sunday, why are you packing so early?"

"I am not a procrastinator. By packing most of my things now, I won't have to worry about forgetting anything."

"If you say so," Lyriq shrugged. "Well, I'm going to make reservations at this great restaurant for tonight, and I'd love for you to join me and a co-worker for lunch tomorrow. Afterwards, the two of us will drive into L.A. for a little shopping at the Beverly Center. Are you game?"

"Definitely, but make sure that fancy restaurant serves something I can actually pronounce," Constance snarked sarcastically.

A couple of hours later, Ryker returned home and picked the ladies up for diner. He decided to forego the reservations Lyriq had made and instead went to a famous eatery that specialized in soul food. He knew his mom well and knew that she would appreciate and seriously critique the food. He was right. With every bite, Constance moaned her approval and pointed out what the chef could've done differently. In her mind, no one could out cook her, but she still gave much praise for the Memphis hot chicken, collard greens, yams, cornbread, and fried okra. She was so full that she had to take the peach cobbler to go. Once they'd returned home and everyone had settled in for the night, Constance found herself sneaking back to the kitchen to grab her cobbler. After eating all that, she knew she'd have to get back on her regular exercise routine once she returned home. She may have been older, but she still wanted to stay fine.

It was no surprise to anyone that Ryker had gotten up and headed into the office to work the first half of Saturday. Constance and Lyriq decided to forego breakfast and just have coffee since they would be meeting Carolyn fairly early for lunch. By twelve-thirty, they were cruising down the boulevard, headed to an eatery Carolyn swore had the best brunch menu in town. After introductions were made and the food arrived, the ladies determined that Carolyn did not lie. The crepes, candied bacon, and other menu items they sampled were all delicious. Constance was glad to see how easily conversation flowed between Carolyn and Lyriq. It gave her hope that the two had made a genuine connection and would be able to grow close in friendship. Lyriq needed someone who was normal, not tainted by the drug world, someone she could relate to professionally that would hopefully be a positive light in her life.

Someone other than family. Lord knows everyone needs one true friend in their life, that proverbial ride or die and Constance hoped Carolyn would become that for Lyriq. After a couple of hours of feasting and laughing, the ladies exchanged hugs and parted ways. Constance and Lyriq blared Kirk Franklin's XM praise station as they headed for the Beverly Center.

Ryker and Lyriq had taken Constance to L.A. for sightseeing before, but she was still looking around as if she was seeing everything for the first time. Her eyes were big with wonderment, and she imagined what the people of Beverly Hills must do for a living to be able to afford to live and shop there. It amazed her how some folks could live so lavishly, while others struggled to find shelter or their next meal. They parked at the Beverly Center, and she prepared herself to look but not touch, because she knew the prices would be well beyond her small-town budget.

"Are you ready to spend a little bit, Constance?" Lyriq winked.

"I'm ready to look at you spend. I'll just be window shopping."

They took the escalators up and landed in Macy's. They looked around but decided to keep moving. The went in and out of boutiques, stopping to look in Gucci and Prada. Lyriq laughed as Constance shook her head at the outrageously priced goods. When they came to Bath & Body Works, Constance grabbed Lyriq by the hand and pulled her inside.

Stacey Covington-Lee

"Now this is my kind of shopping. I know there are things in here I can actually afford," Constance declared as she grabbed a couple of her favorite hand lotions and air fresheners. She went to grab a couple of candles, but Lyriq stopped her.

"Constance, there's a black, female owned company out of Atlanta called Intentional and Pure, they make candles like you've never seen or smelled. I swear, it's like inhaling heaven. I'm going to order you some and they'll be at your door by Tuesday."

"Are they like the ones you've been burning in the condo?"

"Yes, ma'am."

"Oh goodness, then I'll definitely wait on those. Thank you, baby." Constance smiled like a kid getting a special treat for being on their best behavior.

After paying for their items, they exited the store and Constance was almost knocked down by some guy and his girl. Constance gasped and Lyriq barked, "Excuse you! You should watch where you're going before you hurt someone."

"Who you talking to, wench?" The guy's heavy voice spat.

Lyriq turned from Constance to see Craig giving her a death stare as he tightly gripped Bailey's arm. Bailey looked so fragile and pained under the weight of his control.

"Bailey, are you ok?" Lyriq asked, ignoring Craig.

He Won't Go

"She's fine and I won't tell you again to stay out of my business," Craig said with a slight jump in Lyriq's direction as if he were going to pounce on her. When she jumped with fear, he licked his lips and warned, "Next time you won't wake up." He stomped off, dragging Bailey with him.

"Are you okay?" Constance asked with a shaky voice.

"Yes," Lyriq replied as she wiped tears from her cheek. "Are you? He almost knocked you down."

"I'm fine. Wasn't he the guy from the church parking lot the other day? The one Ryker wanted to confront?"

"Yes, and that was my friend, Bailey. He hurt her really badly the day he drugged me, and it looks like he's still causing her immeasurable pain."

"I don't mean to sound cold, Lyriq, but as much as you may care for her, you can't concern yourself with her right now. He is dangerous and you've got to protect yourself. You know what they say, self-preservation is good for the soul. In this case, it's essential for your survival," Constance warned. "Now, let's get out of here before we see them again."

"No," Lyriq said in the most indignant tone she could muster. "We came here to shop and that's what we're going to do. I will not let him send me running out of here like some coward. He will not rule my life." She bent down to retrieve the bags they'd dropped. "You ready to carry on?"

"Yes, I am," Constance affirmed with a rebellious twist of her neck.

The pair moved from store to store, looking at everything from clothes to housewares. Their last stop before leaving was Bloomingdales. Lyriq smiled as she watched Constance try on fancy hats and ogle the jewelry. While the sales lady kept Constance pre-occupied with rings and bangles, Lyriq slipped off and paid for the expensive hat Constance had thrown a fit over. When she returned to her mother-in-law's side, she asked if she was ready to head back.

"Yes. All this walking has left me a little tired. Think I'll have time for a nap before dinner tonight?"

"Of course, you will. Our reservations aren't until eight."

As they headed back towards the escalator in Macy's, Constance quizzed, "What's in the bag? I didn't see you really eye balling anything in Bloomingdale's."

"I didn't but you did. I got you that hat you were drooling over," Lyriq giggled.

"Really? Oh my goodness, I appreciate it, Lyriq but it's so expensive. I can't let you spend that kind of money on me."

"Well, I already did, and folks back home will be speechless when you burst through the church doors with it crowning your head."

He Won't Go

When they reached the car and placed the bags in the trunk, Constance turned to Lyriq and embraced her tightly. "Thank you."

"It was my pleasure."

CHAPTER 31

While Constance napped, Lyriq filled Ryker in on the events that had taken place at the mall. She expressed how fearful she was for Bailey and acknowledged that despite her concern, she knew she had to stay away. Bailey would have to fight this battle on her own.

Furious, Ryker paced the floor. How was he, as a man, as a husband, supposed to let this animal get away with threatening his wife? His spirit was unsettled, and his anger was boiling over. "This isn't right, baby. I don't think I can continue to let this go. There's no way in hell I'm going to have you looking over your shoulder every time you leave, scared of this fool's threats or what he might do next," Ryker huffed, his anger palpable. "I know they said not to call the cops, but letting this go, I don't see how I can do it."

"You have to, Ryker. If we snitch on him, he's got other goons like that big dude, Bishop, that will be happy to kill us in retaliation. Confronting him or reporting him is equivalent to us signing our own death certificates. We have a good life and California is a big state, the likelihood of us running into him again is nil to none."

"I hear you, I...I just need a minute. I've got to clear my head. I'll be back by the time Mama wakes up for dinner."

"Where are you going, Ryker?" Lyriq quizzed with concern in her eyes.

He Won't Go

"For a walk, I just need a little air, babe. I promise, I'm only going around the block and back." Ryker snatched up his keys and cell phone and stomped out the door.

Lyriq plopped down on the couch with her head in her hands. What mess had she created? How had an innocent friendship landed her and her family in the midst of such chaos? She thought she'd left drugs and all the drama and danger that accompanied them back in Georgia, but here she was, dealing with the same enemy again. Only this time, she'd managed to drag her husband in the gutter with her. As she went to wipe the tears from her eyes, she felt Constance sit beside her and gently place a tissue in her hand.

"I heard Ryker leave. He's just frustrated, sweetheart. Don't internalize his anger, it's not directed at you. He knows like I do, none of this is your fault. You didn't purposely set out to get involved with these people. Circumstance brought Bailey and her drama to your door and like any decent man, Ryker wants to protect his wife from the drama," Constance tried to reason.

Lyriq sniffed and shifted her body to look directly into Constance's eye's. "But it is my fault. I have to take responsibility. I never should've called that drug dealer. I never should've caved to that temptation. Bailey tried to protect me from him, but I went behind her back and contacted him. After that initial fall, I should've listened to my husband and not intervened in Baily's drama, but I did and here we are. I appreciate you trying to make me feel better, but your complete honesty is what I need."

"Then yes, you screwed up," Constance stated without apology. "I watched Ryker's father play these kinds of life and death games for years and we know how it turned out for him. Ryker is afraid you'll face the same fate, and reasonably so. He adores you, and not being able to protect you is a hard pill for him to swallow."

Lyriq broke down into uncontrollable sobs. Constance held her in her arms and rocked her like a baby. She stroked Lyriq's hair and hummed the song, "You Know My Name", beautifully as she continued to comfort her daughter-in-law. After the first verse, Lyriq joined her and began to sing, *And oh how He walks with me. Yes, oh how He talks with me. And oh, how he tells me that I am His own.* The pair sang, cried, and praised. It was what Lyriq needed, it reminded her that with all her faults, she was still a child of The Most High.

Ryker walked the streets around the building and as he contemplated his options, he called Kane. He knew his friend would be the voice of reason, the calm in the midst of his storm.

"Hey brother man, what's up," Kane answered in his predicably steady voice.

"I need you to talk me off the ledge, man." Ryker said before recounting the day's events. "I want nothing more than to take this punk's head off. I hate the thought of Lyriq having to always look over her shoulder, scared of who she might bump into. I hate knowing that at any time, this fool could snap and have us hurt or killed just for the thrill of it. How am I supposed to not report him?"

He Won't Go

"Reporting him would put a bigger target on your back, bruh. He is about the streets and wouldn't think twice about having you and Lyriq taken out in order to save his own sorry ass." Kane didn't bite his tongue, he wanted Ryker to know beyond a shadow of a doubt the kind of person he was dealing with. "The best thing you can do is ignore him. He has a short attention span and as long you guys stay out of his sights and Lyriq stays out of his business, he'll move on, forgetting all about the both of you."

"Is that what happened with you? I know you used to use. When you got clean, did you just cut him out of your life?"

"Make no mistake," Kane spoke firmly, "That SOB was never in my life. He was just my father's bastard child. My dad knew early on he was destined for trouble. I think even his mom knew. My dad took care of him, but never tried to cultivate a relationship between us. So, like I said, stay out of his sights and his business."

Ryker signed deeply. "I know you're right, but my soul wants so badly to choke him out."

"Well, tell your soul to calm down. He is not worth your life and stop allowing him to steal your peace," Kane spoke in a commanding voice. "You're always talking about God, well, let God deal with him."

Shocked, Ryker did a double take at the phone and then eased it back to his ear. "If you're bringing God into this, then clearly I need to leave it alone."

"Yeah, I've been hearing a lot of God talk this past forty-eight hours. My dad has just revealed to the family that he has terminal cancer. He's known for a while, but didn't tell anyone, not even my mom. I've been over here with them and a few other family members, reminiscing and loving on one another. It's amazing how having death looming over you will make you want to rededicate your life to God and spend time with the family that in years before, couldn't pay you to stay home with them."

"Kane, man, I'm so sorry. I know y'all have had a rocky relationship, but he's still your dad. The love is still there."

"Yeah, so it seems. I'm not ready to let the old man go. Despite his mistakes, he still has a lot of redeeming qualities, and I can't deny that he was always a heck of a provider. We never went without, never wanted for anything."

"Is there anything I can do for you, Kane?"

"Yeah, don't laugh or run and hide under the pews when you see me walk into that church of yours tomorrow. Apparently, Dad convinced my mom that after all these years, Victory Land is where they belong. They asked me to accompany them, and I couldn't say no."

"As long as the floors don't start shaking and the columns don't crumble, I'll stand with a straight face," Ryker joked.

Back at the condo, Lyriq had made the executive decision to not go out for dinner. She and Constance riffled through take-out menus,

He Won't Go

trying to decide what they'd have delivered. As Constance read a menu from a Chinese place, Lyriq looked at her with tears in her eyes. She'd been raised to respect her elders, to always treat them with honor and she recognized she had fallen short when it came to Constance.

"Why are you tearing up now?" Constance quizzed.

"I'm still trying to understand what brought about this change of heart for you. I know you were concerned when Ryker and me started dating, and even more so when we married. I know I'm not who or what you wanted for your son. When Ryker told me you had come to town, I expected you to spend all of your time trying to convince Ryker to send me back to Georgia. I expected you tell me how I was never good enough for your son. But all you've done is love me. Even in the face of me not giving you the respect you deserve. Somewhere along the line, I went from being respectful and calling you Ms. Constance to just Constance. As if you were my age and not my elder. As if you hadn't earned the respect of a proper title. I am so sorry," Lyriq sniffed.

Constance passed her a tissue. "My son loves you and I came to the realization that if I want to continue as a valued part of his life, I had to accept his wife. I never had anything against you, but it was hard to not think of the consequences your past life could have on Ryker's future. But after you two announced you were married, your past didn't matter. You are his and he is yours. I know the man I raised, and I know he will never leave you, despite how hard it gets.

He simply won't go, so I had no choice but to embrace you, to support you, and wrap you in love. As far as titles, yes, I earned mine. I've earned your respect and I accept your apology."

"Thank you, Ms. Constance." Lyriq threw her arms around Constance's neck and placed a sweet kiss on her cheek.

Ryker had just opened the door and he stood there watching the exchange between his bride and his mother. He thanked God for letting peace and love abide between them.

Constance looked up. "What are you doing sneaking around, boy?" She joked.

"Watching what I'd prayed for but wasn't sure I'd witness. A blossoming love between the two most important people in my life."

"Enough of the mushy stuff, what's in the bag, man?" Lyriq smirked.

"I hope y'all don't mind, but I'm not up for going out, so I walked to that Chinese place down the block."

"Perfect," the ladies yelped in unison.

"Apparently, you've become a mind reader," Lyriq smiled as she stood to take the bags and set up the food. She pulled box after box of shrimp, noodles, chicken, fried rice, Hunan beef, and spring rolls from the bag. She poured glasses of sweet tea and set the table with plates and silverware. That evening, the three of them laughed and ate as if they didn't have a care in the world.

CHAPTER 32

Constance packed the last of her things in her carry-on bag. She moved to the full-length mirror, smoothed her lovely navy-blue dress, and straightened her pearls. Satisfied with her appearance, she retrieved her clutch purse and Bible. As she walked out of the bedroom, she called to Ryker, "My bags are all ready to go down, baby."

"Okay, Mom, I'll come and get them in just a minute." Ryker finished straightening the knot in his tie. He smoothed his hand over his shirt as he looked beyond his own reflection in the mirror to admire his wife's free flowing hair and beautiful, fitted, purple dress. It was cinched at the waist with a wide black, leather belt and the six-inch black heels made her calf muscles pop in a way that drove men crazy. She looked like perfection.

"What are you staring at, old man?" Lyriq asked with a sly grin.

"The woman I plan to make love to tonight," he replied with a mannish grin of his own.

Lyriq walked over to him seductively, leaned in and planted a juicy kiss om his lips. "You'd better go help your mother before we both get in trouble."

With a low moan, Ryker turned away and headed down the hall to the room his mother had been occupying. "Okay, Mamma, is this everything you've got?" He asked, and grabbed the handles of her luggage.

"Yep, that's everything," Constance confirmed as she handed him a Kleenex. "Now wipe that plum lipstick from your mouth."

"Oh, thank you, ma'am."

After cleaning his face, Ryker lugged the bags to the front door and bellowed for the women to come on. A couple of minutes later, they headed down to the garage, got situated in the car, and headed to Victory Land. When they arrived, Deacon Roosevelt spotted them and instructed one of the parking attendants to give them one of the reserved spots near the entrance.

Deacon Roosevelt made haste to the passenger door where Constance was seated. He opened the door for her, sang a cheerful "Good morning" to everyone, while extending his arm to offer Constance an escort. Ryker and Lyriq exchanged quizzical glances as he stretched his hand to assist her out of the car. They looked on curiously as they followed the deacon and Constance, wondering when the two had become so familiar with one another. The pair chatted and giggled like reunited sweethearts. Once they'd taken their seats and the deacon had moved on, Ryker leaned over and asked Constance when she'd become so chummy with Deacon Roosevelt.

"After that meeting we all had here the other week, Roosevelt and I exchanged numbers and we've been speaking on the phone every night since," she blushed. "Did you know he's originally from Warner Robins? Imagine that; he's good old country folk like us. Practically neighbors back home."

Ryker was speechless. He had no clue the pair had shared any more than a polite hello. He looked at Lyriq as if to ask if she knew. Lyriq frowned and shook her head. She was just as surprised and clueless as Ryker. The deacons started devotion and Ryker put thoughts of his mom and Deacon Roosevelt on the back burner. After an old-time hymn and a prayer, the deacons took their seats and the choir stood to serenade the congregation. Ryker listened intently as Lyriq sang along with the choir. Her voice was phenomenal, and it never took more than a note from her to get him swept up in a song, swept up in emotion. Lyriq stopped singing and nudged Ryker, pulling him out of his lyrical trance. Kane, his mother, and father were easing into the pew in front of them. Kane greeted them with a broad smile and offered Ryker a strong handshake.

The choir sang another song as Pastor Carlton made his way to the pulpit. He went and knelt on one knee in front of his chair and prayed while the choir continued to usher in the Holy Spirit with song. A few seconds later, he stood and began to clap in rhythm with the rest of the church. As the song came to a close, Pastor Carlton could be heard bellowing through the sound system.

Stacey Covington-Lee

"Let the church say amen! Thank you, choir, for blessing us this morning. Church, this is the day that The Lord has made, let us rejoice and be glad in it."

The congregation clapped and offered up Amens and Halleluiahs.

Pastor Carlton placed his tablet on the podium and powered it up, ready to deliver The Word. But when he started to speak, he suddenly paused and looked as if something was suddenly weighing heavily on him. "Church, sometimes something hits your heart, and it simply cannot be ignored. God has placed it on my heart to ask our beautiful sister, Lyriq Adams, to bless us with a song."

Lyriq started shrinking into the pew, hoping it would swallow her whole. She hadn't sung for a crowd in months. She had not prepared for this. She started praying Pastor Carlton would revoke his request and move on with his sermon. But he did no such thing.

"Lyriq, I apologize for putting you on the spot, but when The Lord instructs me, I obey. Please join me up here and bless us in your own way. Church, give her hand of encouragement."

The church clapped vigorously for Lyriq. She still looked petrified, but eased a bit when Ryker whispered, "I'll be by your side the whole time." He then stood and held his hand out for Lyriq. After a couple of beats, she placed her hand in his and they walked to the pulpit. As promised, Ryker stood right beside her. Lyriq took the microphone one of the assistants offered.

He Won't Go

"Bear with me, church, I haven't done this in a while." Lyriq then looked at Pastor Carlton and teased, "I'll wait patiently for God's instruction on how to pay you back for this one, Pastor." She and the congregation shared a chuckle. "Lately, I've found myself going through trials and tribulations that I thought were behind me, but this song has helped me tremendously and I hope it helps you as well." She took a deep breath and began to sing acapella. *Take me to the king, I don't have much to bring. My heart is torn to pieces, it's my offering.* Her voice carried through the church like it was riding on the wings of angels. She didn't hear the pianist when he joined her serenade. She didn't feel when Ryker stepped out of her spotlight. She didn't hear the cries and shouts from the congregation that was remarkably moved by her talent or the weeping from her mother-in-law who saw the potential of who Lyriq could be in The Lord. Lyriq sang her last note, opened her eyes and saw the church on their feet. Applause and shouts rang out, the spirit was truly moving through that place. She looked to her left and saw her husband wipe tears as he walked towards her with open arms.

As they returned to their seats, Pastor Carlton proclaimed, "That is why we must obey our Master's instruction. When we don't, we miss His blessings." Again, Pastor Carlton clicked on his tablet, but this time he brought forth The Word. He spoke with authority, with passion, and conviction. It was easy to see how his congregation had grown large in number and powerful in faith. As he brought the sermon to a close, Pastor Carlton opened the doors to the church. "If The Lord spoke to you today, if something we did or said touched

221

your heart, and you find yourself looking for a church home, we extend an invitation to you right now to become part of our Victory Land family. Walk down this aisle and we'll meet you with open arms and open hearts."

The church clapped and praised as two families and another woman with her child walked down the aisle, gave their lives to Christ, and became part of the Victory Land family. After Pastor Carlton prayed over them, they were ushered to the back for further instruction. Pastor Carlton then turned and faced Kane and his parents. "Church family, please be patient with us as we invite one of our new families, the Garrisons, to join me up front for a special prayer. Kane Garrison Sr. is facing a difficult battle and needs our prayers and our strength. We need to come together and stand in the gap for this family. Please, Garrison family, join me now," Pastor Carlton said with an outstretched hand.

As Kane and his parents made it to the altar, they realized someone else was walking down the aisle. The look on Pastor Carlton's face made it clear that whomever it was wasn't invited or welcomed. Everyone turned to see Craig hastily walking with Ms. Betty pulling at him, trying to stop his journey to the front. Standing guard at the door was big dude, beside him was Bailey, holding her daughter, glancing around as if she were mapping out an escape route.

"Craig please, this isn't the time or place," Ms. Betty pleaded.

He Won't Go

Craig stopped long enough to take his mother by the hand and reassure her. "Mom, we're family too and we're going to pray for my father like everyone else." They took a few more steps and stopped at Kane Sr.'s side. Craig glanced over at Kane and smirked, "What's up, brother?"

With tears of shame and embarrassment running down her face, Ms. Betty mumbled her apologies to those that stood at the front of the church.

"Mom, you have nothing to apologize for. Isn't that right, Dad? I mean, I know you're up here with your real family, but I am your son too! You didn't do right by my mom, but we don't hold grudges, do we, Mom? We're here to pray for you like everyone else."

Kane made a move towards his brother, but his father placed a hand in the center of his chest to stop him. "No son, if this is what they want to do, let them. Please, Pastor Carlton, let's continue."

"Yeah, Pastor, go on and pray, lay hands or whatever it is you do," Craig retorted.

The entire congregation looked on in shock and disbelief at the scene unfolding before them. But when Pastor Carlton began to pray, almost everyone fell in line and bowed their heads in prayer as well. Instead of praying, Lyriq looked on in fear and Ryker in anger. Lyriq kept glancing back at Bailey, she was more afraid for her than she was for herself. Bailey looked like she wanted to run, but big dude side-eyed her as if to say, "Don't even think about it." So instead, she stood there bouncing her daughter on her hip.

After the prayer, Pastor Carlton dismissed church and watched all of the parishioners get ushered out through the back doors, past Bailey and big dude. At one point, Bailey tried to blend in with the throng of people and ease out, but she didn't get far before she was snatched back. She was pushed down onto a pew and in the process, her daughter's head hit the side of the seat and the little girl began to cry.

Ms. Betty again offered her apologies to Kane, his father, and especially his mother. "I had no idea that this is what my son had in mind when he suggested we come to church. Ma'am, I never meant to hurt you or disrespect your marriage, and I certainly didn't mean for any of this to happen." She then turned and scurried down the aisle to check on her granddaughter.

"You should be apologizing to her, old man. You used her and threw her away."

Kane's father did not reply. Instead, he took his wife by the hand and led her out of the church.

"So, you're just going to turn your back and walk away from me like I'm invisible? Like you don't hear me talking to you? Nobody turns their back on me, old man," Craig barked as he took off behind his father. And that's when Kane and Ryker jumped into action.

CHAPTER 33

The commotion had moved from the sanctuary to the parking lot. Big dude had given Ms. Betty the key to his car and watched as she, Bailey, and the baby got safely inside. He then ran to be by Craig's side, ready to take out whoever stepped to them. Pastor Carlton called the police before running outside, while Deacon Roosevelt ushered Constance to his car to keep her safe from danger. Just as he opened the door for her, Kane and Craig came tumbling out the church doors. Kane quickly got to his feet and Craig swung on him again, but Ryker grabbed Craig's arm, preventing the punch from landing. That's when big dude tackled Ryker as if they were on a football field. Constance screamed out but was pushed on into the car before she could take a step towards the commotion.

"Stay put," Deacon Roosevelt commanded as he hastily walked towards the fight.

Pastor Carlton stepped in the middle of the melee, attempting to separate the four men. He'd barely laid a hand on Craig's shoulder before he was punched. To everyone's surprise, even his own, Pastor Carlton swung back and connected with Craig's jaw. Craig went down but when he came back up, he was brandishing a gun. He shot off a round and everyone scattered, ducking behind cars, screaming and praying for their safety. Big dude stood behind Craig while Kane, Ryker, and Pastor Carlton all raised their hands and slowly took a few steps back.

Fear gripped Constance. She looked on in horror as Lyriq slowly stepped in front of Ryker. She took a couple more steps, moving closer to Craig. "The cops are on their way. Just leave. No one needs to die here today. You just prayed for your father on this Holy ground, do you now want to commit murder on the same Holy ground?"

"I've told you to stay out of my business," Craig barked as he leveled the gun down, aiming it right at Lyriq's chest.

Ryker moved to protect Lyriq and Constance's fear over took her. She had to do something; she could not lose her beloved son.

An enraged Craig looked as if he'd become possessed. Anger and evil burned in his eyes as he proclaimed, "I'm going to kill all of you!"

He aimed the gun at Ryker. Deacon Roosevelt attempted to push Ryker out of the line of fire, but the tires screeched, and he was side swiped by the car's fender. Deacon Roosevelt was knocked to the side, but the car kept going. Big dude jumped out the way and the car barreled forward until it connected head-on with Craig. People watched in disbelief and horror as he flew over the hood, pounded into the windshield, and rolled lifelessly onto the concrete. The car stopped, the driver's door flew open, and a wailing Ms. Betty

He Won't Go

practically fell from the driver's seat and crawled on the ground to her son. She lifted Craig's head to her lap and sobbed. Bailey, in a complete state of shock, sat in the back seat, rocking her baby girl.

"I'm so sorry, son. Please forgive me. You're my baby and I love you so much. God forgive me. Please Lord, let my baby be okay. Please don't leave me, son." Ms. Betty begged God and Craig for forgiveness and for him to be spared. "I'm so sorry. I couldn't let you kill anyone, baby, but please God, don't let me have killed my baby. Oh, Jesus have mercy." Her sobs were heart wrenching.

Kane watched as his father moved to be at his other son's side. Kane Sr. knelt down with tears rolling down his face. He wrapped an arm around Ms. Betty's shoulder and caressed Craig's face. "Come on, son, stay with us."

The sirens blared as the cop cars turned onto the church property. Thankfully, they were followed by an ambulance. Police got out with guns drawn and everyone raised their hands in surrender. Pastor Carlton approached slowly, identifying himself and telling them that the threat was down, and medical assistance was needed. After one officer secured the gun Craig had been brandishing, they allowed the emergency medical technicians to render aid to Craig and Deacon Roosevelt. Another ambulance was called and both men were rushed to the hospital.

The officers proceeded to get statements from everyone on the scene. They attempted to get a statement from Ms. Betty, but she was too distraught to speak. All she wanted was to be at her son's side.

Stacey Covington-Lee

Pastor Carlton told them he would take full responsibility for Ms. Betty and would make sure she was available to talk to them, if they'd just let her go be with her son. Thankfully, they obliged, and Kane and his parents escorted her to the hospital.

Ryker was comforting his mother, while Lyriq offered comfort and reassurance to Bailey. When Ryker called her name, Lyriq took Bailey by the hand and pulled her along. Bailey kept staring at big dude, waiting for him to stop her from walking away, but with the cops still on the scene, he just stood there with his head down. With his car being used to run down Craig, the cops needed to search it. When they found a gun and bags full of pills and weed in the console, big dude turned and tried to flee the scene, but one cop pulled his Taser and stopped big dude in his tracks. He was the only one to be arrested at the scene.

Tears of relief ran down Bailey's face. She didn't know Craig's fate, but in that moment, she felt a rush of relief and freedom wash over her. She wept as she hugged her baby close.

CHAPTER 34

Ryker and Lyriq rushed Constance and Bailey to the hospital. Constance needed to know that Roosevelt was okay, while Bailey needed to know if she was truly free or if she would still be a slave to Craig. They entered the emergency room and saw a still weeping Ms. Betty being consoled by both of Kane's parents. The kindness and empathy Kane's mother displayed in that moment, under those circumstances, was remarkable. Not many women would've been able to put past hurts and betrayals aside, in order to provide comfort to the ones that hurt them. But forgiveness was a powerful thing and she'd forgiven a long time ago. It's the reason she could be this strong and supportive in this moment.

"I couldn't let him shoot anyone, but how could I have hit my own child? What have I done?" Ms. Betty rocked and cried.

"God knows your heart, He knows..." Mrs. Garrison said in an attempt to comfort her husband's ex-mistress.

"Has anyone said anything about Deacon Roosevelt?" Constance asked anxiously. In that moment, she quite honestly didn't care about Craig, she had tunnel vision and only wanted an update on the deacon. He was the one she'd been speaking with every night, the one who had made her feel like a woman again. He was the one she was smitten with. In that moment, under those circumstances,

Craig was just the animal that threatened her family and forced his poor mother into actions she'd normally never consider.

"No, we're waiting on word about Deacon Roosevelt and Craig. The nurse promised we'd here from the doctors soon," Pastor Carlton assured.

While they waited for what seemed an eternity, a couple of cops and detectives showed up to take statements from everyone that had been at the church. They started with Pastor Carlton, then the Garrisons, Ryker and his family, and then Bailey. When they went to question Ms. Betty, Pastor Carlton stepped forward and told them that would only speak to them in the presence of her attorney. Ms. Betty looked up with furrowed brow.

"I don't have an attorney," Ms. Betty whimpered.

"Yes, you do, and he'll be here shortly," Pastor Carlton assured her. "I just want to make sure you're as protected as you can possibly be throughout this ordeal."

"Thank you," Ms. Betty said as she gave Pastor Carlton's hand a slight squeeze.

"We still need a statement, or we'll have to take her down to the station," One of detectives retorted.

Before anyone could reply, a well-dressed young man carrying a briefcase, stepped forward and inserted, "I'm sure there's a conference room or empty waiting room here we can use. That way, my client can continue to wait on word about her son."

He Won't Go

"And who are you?" The detective asked with a voice full of annoyance.

"I'm her attorney, Maxwell Banks. Now let me locate a room, have a moment with my client, and we'll be glad to speak with you."

Maxwell turned and walked to the reception desk to inquire about a room. As he walked away, one of the emergency room doctors approached the group and asked if the family of Roosevelt Hayes was there. Pastor Carlton and Constance both stepped forward. Pastor Carlton explained their relationship and explained they were the closest thing Roosevelt had to family.

"Well, I'm pleased to tell you that Mr. Hayes will be just fine. He suffered a few scrapes and a broken leg, but a few weeks in a cast followed by a little rehab, and he should be like new," the doctor smiled warmly. "He's really lucky, at his age, this could've been a lot worse."

"May I please see him?" Constance asked.

"Of course, follow me. He's had some pain meds so he may be a little groggy," the doctor warned.

Both Constance and Pastor Carlton entered the room to see Deacon Roosevelt laid up with his leg cast and elevated on pillows. He turned his head to see his visitors and a broad smile crossed his face at the sight of Constance. Pastor Carlton looked between the two and decided he'd come back after the deacon and Constance had time to visit alone.

"Who told you to try and be a hero?" Constance teased.

"The crazy man in my head. Next time, I'll tell him to shut up," Deacon Roosevelt chuckled.

Constance moved to his side, sat on the edge of the bed and took his hand in hers. They talked and comforted one another. She assured him he'd be fine, and the conversation moved to how they could be there to take care of one another.

Back in the waiting room, everyone continued to hold vigil, waiting on news about Craig. Each one secretly holding on to what their hope was for his outcome. After about an hour-long interview, Betty was allowed to rejoin the others to wait for news on her son. Her attorney and the detectives made their exit, with the detectives promising to stop back by once word of Craig's condition became available. It was another hour before a surgeon finally emerged from the back with word about Craig's condition and prognosis. He explained that the angle and impact of the hit, severed Craig's spinal cord. He also suffered head trauma when he hit the ground and there had been significant bleeding in his brain. The doctor emphasized that if Craig survived the night, he'd forever be a paraplegic.

Ms. Betty collapsed in the arms of Pastor Carlton and wept like a wounded animal. "What have I done?" She moaned. "My baby... Oh God, my baby boy." Her pain was palpable.

There was no denying the pain everyone felt for Ms. Betty and the reality of her situation. However, what each person felt for Craig

232

himself was quite different. Although Pastor Carlton felt a pang of guilt over his new-found sense of freedom, Bailey felt no guilt. She only felt the freedom of Craig's heaviness being lifted from her life. He no longer had the power to be the suffocating, controlling presence he'd been in her life for so long. Lyriq felt a sense of relief for Bailey and one of security for herself, knowing that Craig could never drug, threaten, or hurt her again. She looked at Ryker and knew he shared that same sense of security. The Garrisons, for the most part, felt nothing. Kane Sr. was of course hurt that this was his son's fate, but he also recognized that no man could live the life Craig had lived and make it out unscathed. Maybe if he'd been a faithful husband, a better father, none of this would've happened. But it was too late now for should've, could've, would've.

Ms. Betty was allowed to stay at her son's side in the ICU that night. She held his hand, apologized, prayed over him, read scripture, begged and bartered with God, but none of that was enough to save Craig. He was pronounced dead at four forty-five a.m.

CHAPTER 35

Three months after Craig's passing found everyone pressing forward with their lives, including Ms. Betty. The police had determined that her actions likely saved the lives of many and opted not to pursue criminal charges. While part of her was relieved she wouldn't face jail time, another part of her thought prison might absolve her of some of the guilt she still felt over killing her only child.

After his funeral services, Ms. Betty went about the business of cleaning out Craig's apartment. In the process, she found a file with her name on it. It contained instructions for a safety deposit box he'd maintained in both their names. The box held the deed to her home, the one she always thought he was just renting for her. It also contained the deed to the apartment building Craig lived in. Turned out, he owned the entire complex. The deeds were in both their names, which meant Ms. Betty now owned it all. There was also a sizable amount of cash, enough that would allow Ms. Betty to retire. But instead, she purchased the café she'd been working at. She'd always wanted to be a business owner and in death, Craig made her dream a reality.

After experiencing their love and support, Ms. Betty sold the apartment complex to the church. Pastor Carlton was establishing it as part of their drug rehabilitation center, in hopes of pulling even more of the community out of the despair of addition. The bulk of the proceeds she received from the sale of the apartments she gave to Bailey, along with her heartfelt apologies for how poorly she'd treated her over the years. She acknowledged the pain Craig had inflicted upon Bailey and sincerely asked for forgiveness. For the sake of her daughter, Bailey forgave Ms. Betty and the two worked to build a better relationship.

With the money she'd been gifted, Bailey purchased a lovely home for she and her baby girl. She also decided to go back to school and complete her degree. She wanted an opportunity to experience the same sense of fulfillment and pride she saw Lyriq experiencing through her teaching career.

Constance had delayed her trip back home by two weeks after the events in the church parking lot, only to return two months later. She wasn't coming to her son and daughter-in-law's rescue this time though. Instead, she was coming to collect her man. With she and Roosevelt both widowed and caring so much for one another in such a short time span, they decided to make it official and marry after the upcoming church services. Then they'd pack his home and drive cross-country, back to Georgia.

Lyriq and Ryker's relationship was stronger than ever. They'd sought counseling through a Christian therapist to strengthen their bond and better understand how they could continue to deal with drug addiction as a unit, always supporting each other without judgement or finger pointing. They were learning, growing, and preparing for the possibility of expanding their family. Ryker and Kane continued to generate new business for the firm, while Lyriq grew as a teacher and mentor. She was becoming so much more than she ever thought she could be. She'd also become a permanent part of the church choir, helping to usher in The Holy Spirit every Sunday morning and Ryker could not be prouder.

~~~

Walking through the halls of the school, Carolyn and Lyriq chatted about their weekend plans. Carolyn sharing how she planned to have a weekend of self-care with a massage, manicure, and pedicure and beyond that, she'd spend her time binging on *Bridgerton*.

"Well, while you're looking at fictional folks fall in love, I'll be witnessing my mother-in-law tie the knot after church on Sunday."

"That's so sweet. She deserves this chance to be happy and in love again. It's been a long time since her husband died, right?" Carolyn quizzed.

"Yes, many years. No one should be alone that long. And she's marrying a great guy," Lyriq said, before having her attention snatched away by a couple of seemingly misbehaving kids. She watched as a fourth grader snatched something from another boy and yell in his face. "Excuse me, Carolyn."

Lyriq approached the boys and asked, "What is going on over here? What are you all tussling over?" She asked as she reached for the boys' hand. The boys panicked, one dropped something on the floor and they both took off running. Lyriq exhaled her annoyance as she bent down to retrieve the dropped item. It was a small baggie of pills, Oxycontin to be exact and Lyriq knew their power well. She looked around to find that everyone had disappeared into their respective classrooms. She knew she should've taken the bag of pills straight to the principal and she didn't know why, but instead she tucked them in her pocket and returned to her class. When school was over, she popped her truck and tucked the little baggie under a corner of the carpeted floorboard. She closed the trunk, jumped in the driver's seat and sped away.

The weekend was full of laughter and celebration. Lyriq spent Saturday with Constance, being pampered and making the bride-to-be feel special as she prepared to exchange vows with her sweetie. Saturday evening was spent with a house full of friends and church family eating, laughing, and enjoying time with the happy couple that would soon leave them for the red clay dirt of Georgia.

After everyone had departed, Lyriq knocked on Constance's door. "May I come in?"

"Of course," Constance replied.

Lyriq joined her on the bed. "Are you excited about tomorrow? Ready for your single life to forever change?"

"You know, baby, I never imagined I'd marry again. I thought I'd live out the rest of my days alone, but it looks like God had other plans and I couldn't be more excited. That old house gets awfully lonely sometimes, so yes, I'm ready. I'm ready to share my time and space with Roosevelt. He's a good man and I know we'll bring each other a lot of joy in these golden years."

"You deserve every bit of the happiness coming your way," Lyriq smiled as she dabbed at a tear in the corner of her eye. "Anyway, I wanted to bring you a little gift, something new for your big day," Lyriq said as she held out a small jewelry box. Inside were a pair of perfect two-karat, diamond drop earrings. "I think these will go beautifully with your dress."

This time it was Constance that dabbed at tears. "They are gorgeous. Thank you."

"You're welcome. And now I'm going to bed, we've got an early go in the morning and seven o'clock will roll around faster than I expect it to. Goodnight, Ms. Constance."

"Goodnight, Lyriq. I love you."

Lyriq smiled and closed the door behind her. She thanked God for softening Constance's heart towards her and allowing them to build a loving, mutually respectful relationship.

"What are you smiling about?" Ryker asked as Lyriq entered their bedroom.

"I'm just happy, babe. I have a fine, sexy husband that loves me, a mother-in-law who loves me, and a million other reasons to be thankful."

238

He Won't Go

"Well, climb on over here and let me give you something else to be thankful for," Ryker said playfully yet seductively. Without hesitation, Lyriq dove into bed, ready to get all her husband had for her.

The next morning when the doors to the church flung open, Bailey, Ms. Betty, and the Garrisons all joined Ryker, Lyriq, Constance, and Roosevelt for church service and to witness the nuptials that were to follow. The congregation poured in, ready to hear from The Lord. Lyriq and the choir brought the music and Pastor Carlton brought the message. Four more souls were saved that day when a family joined the church and committed their lives to Christ. It was a beautiful thing to witness. And now it was time for the church to witness the exchanging of vows between Constance and Deacon Roosevelt.

With Constance and Roosevelt standing at the front of the church, flanked by Ryker and Lyriq serving as best man and matron of honor, Pastor Carlton asked the church to bow their heads as he prayed over the couple. With a unified "Amen," Pastor Carlton continued with the ceremony, asking both Constance and Roosevelt if they took one another in sickness and health, richer and poorer, forsaking all others. They exchanged rings and shared Holy Communion. It was then that Pastor Carlton declared them husband and wife and invited Deacon Roosevelt to kiss his bride. The church erupted in applause and cheers. When the happy couple turned to make their way down the aisle past the well-wishers, the church door flung open, and they were stopped in their tracks.

Bishop, or as Lyriq called him, big dude stood blocking the door, his face expressionless. He was out of jail, and no one knew if he was there for revenge or redemption.

"Are the doors to the church still open?" Bishop asked. "If so, I'd like to join. I can't continue to live the way I've been living. My soul is tired and God's been talking to me. I know if I don't take this step, if I don't commit my life to God, I'll be dead within the week." He tried to wipe at the tears that had started to flow, but they were coming too fast.

Pastor Carlton walked down the aisle, past the newly married couple. He opened his arms and Bishop fell into his embrace.

"Do you believe that Jesus is the son of God?"

"Yes," Bishop sobbed.

"Do you believe with all of your heart that Jesus died for our sins?"

"Yes," Bishop sniffed.

Pastor Carlton continued, "Will you work with and for this church for the upbuilding of God's kingdom?"

"Yes, I give my word." Bishop said with all sincerity.

"Church, let's welcome our newest member," Pastor Carlton said in a booming voice. "If you've ever doubted God's power to save, doubt no more." The church erupted with shouts of Amen, Hallelujah, and thunderous applause.

As the celebration of Constance and Roosevelt's nuptials, and Bishop's new commitment to God continued in the reception hall, Lyriq snuck out to her car. She popped her trunk, dug out the hidden pills, and crept back in the church. In the bathroom stall, she whispered a prayer and flushed the pills. God had been too good, and had shown her too much grace and mercy for her to risk everything for a temporary high. The joy He'd given her, the happiness that coursed through her body was the only high she needed. She ran back out to her husband's side, more committed than ever to him, their marriage, and her God.

Stacey Covington-Lee

If you or someone you know needs help escaping a domestic violence situation, please call the National Domestic Violence Hotline by phone @ 1-800-799-7233 or text START to 88788.

If you or someone you know is struggling with addiction, please contact the SAMHSA's National Hotline @ 800-662-HELP (4357).

Also Available from SCL Novels

Bitter Taste of Love

Hate The Way He Loves Me

When Love Ain't Enough

The Love That Lies Between Us

and the classic series ~ The Knife In My Back

www.sclnovels.com